Season of Ice

Season of Ice

Diane Les Becquets

BLOOMSBURY

Published by Bloomsbury U.S.A. Children's Books
175 Fifth Avenue, New York, New York 10010
Distributed to the trade by Macmillan

Library of Congress Cataloging-in-Publication Data
Les Becquets, Diane.
Season of ice / Diane Les Becquets.— 1st U.S. ed.
        p.   cm.
Summary: When seventeen-year-old Genesis Sommer's father disappears
on Moosehead Lake near their small-town Maine home in mid-November,
she must cope with the pressure of keeping her family together,
even while rumors about the event plague her.
ISBN-13: 978-1-59990-063-6 • ISBN-10: 1-59990-063-7 (hardcover)
[1. Missing persons—Fiction.   2. Fathers and daughters—Fiction.
3. Stepfamilies—Fiction.   4. Lakes—Fiction.   5. Moosehead Lake (Me.)—
Fiction.   6. Maine—Fiction.]   I. Title.
PZ7.L56245Se 2008   [Fic]—dc22   2007030845

First U.S. Edition 2008
Typeset by Westchester Book Composition
Printed in the U.S.A. by Quebecor World Fairfield
2 4 6 8 10 9 7 5 3 1

For Nate

FALL TURNOVER

CHAPTER

1

In the beginning there was snow. Torrents of tiny flakes blew in off the lake, pricked my skin before they melted on my hands and face and tongue. I live in Sebaticuk, a small town in northern Maine on the shores of Moosehead Lake. I no longer think of that massive body as just water but rather a whale of sorts, a creature that I cannot tame and whose belly I cannot see.

"Gonna have us a doozy," Perry had said that morning. Perry is my uncle. He works at the Dealership in town. The Dealership hasn't sold cars for fifty years. It just fixes them.

This is what happened.

Saturday morning, November 18, four months before I would turn eighteen, six weeks or so before another ice-racing season would begin.

"Genesis, hurry up!"

I was upstairs in the bathroom brushing my teeth. My father was standing at the foot of the stairs.

Why do I remember everything so clearly now? The

rust stains running like crooked streams down the porcelain basin toward the drain, the faint smell of Clorox, the splatters on the mirror, my thoughts. I was debating trimming my hair, cutting off the broken ends, using the toenail clippers from the shelf above the faucet. My hair is long, straight, and brown. My face is fair. "Are you anemic?" people have asked me. "No," I say. Even when it snows so hard that my cheeks sting and my nose burns, my skin remains pale, like cream-colored powder, dampened and smeared.

But I didn't trim my hair. I rinsed my mouth, ran downstairs, and grabbed my coat off the banister. My jacket felt tight that day, like I couldn't breathe, and I wondered if I had gained weight or my breasts had grown.

My father, Mike, was a large man with a fleshy, hopeful face, dull charcoal hair, and deep brown eyes resembling a buck's. His skin always had a sheen to it, especially under the eyes, and a scent as strong as bark and soil and wind, an odor that would wrap itself around me when I kissed him on the cheek. He worked for the Great Northern Timber Company at a Canadian border camp that's a two-hour drive north. Packed all of his hulking six-foot-five, 280-pound body into a twenty-ton Forespro delimber. His job was breaking limbs, snapping off what God put on, and while he could have probably done it for real to people, he was, normally, a meek giant. Four days a week he slept in a camp trailer with other guys who cut and hauled lumber to the paper mills in Millinocket. While he was away, I'd think of him collapsing into his small bunk after a fourteen-hour day, dreaming not of women or daughters or even his childhood, but of trees, their smooth, gray, amputated limbs piled high around him like so much confetti.

When he'd return home after his shift, I'd smell his exhaustion, hear it in his feet as he'd lumber up the stairs to run a bath. Linda would always bring him a brandy. I'd see her pass my room with the small tumbler in her hand, listen to her open and shut the bathroom door. I'd picture her sitting on the toilet seat beside the tub as their voices passed gently between them, slow conversation and occasional laughter. Sometimes I'd hear soft splashing, and I'd imagine Linda washing my father's back or undressing and easing into the water with him.

Linda is my stepmom. She has been with us for almost ten years. Long enough to bring Scott and Alex into the world—eight-year-old twins, who sleep down the hall and could pass for identical, though they're not. In the beginning they were seven, but another birthday has come and gone since then.

I say the beginning because everything before that day in November feels like a dream, like I wasn't really living. My life is different now, each second a deliberate moment, as if the earth's gravitational pull has intensified and every particle of life weighs more.

My father's shifts ran Monday through Thursday. He always had the weekends off. On that particular Saturday morning, Linda was sitting in the kitchen cutting coupons out of the morning paper and talking on the phone to her mother, who lives in New Hampshire. Scott and Alex were watching cartoons. Dad and I left the house and climbed into his pickup, a 1992 GMC that once was silver but now is green, with a black vinyl split-seat patched with duct tape. I straddled strips of sticky residue where the adhesive had melted from days in the sun, smelled the old coffee stains from the mug he kept wedged where the seat splits.

"Perry's got some ideas for your car," Dad said.

"Oh, yeah?"

"Says he's got a nice eight-and-three-quarter differential that will fit right into the rear end. It'll get you traction on both tires at the same time. Give you a clear-cut edge."

Dad and Perry were always brainstorming ideas for my car, a 1993 V6 Mustang, five-speed, 3.8-liter engine. I'd been racing it on the lake the past two winters as part of a local ice-racing club.

Dad pulled up to the Dealership on the corner of Gunnison and Main. Perry's garage was made of cinder blocks painted white, which had dulled over the years and on most days resembled the sky. Piles of gray slush carved with tire treads covered the concrete slab in front of the garage and were beginning to freeze. As we climbed out of the truck, I held my arms out to the sides and took a long glide over a smooth patch of ice.

Inside, Perry had already started working on my car,

prepping it for the upcoming season. He had raised the hood and was changing the spark plugs. A radio was playing hits from the seventies and eighties.

"Hey, Little Bit."

Perry liked to call me Little Bit. I was small. Had never passed much more than five feet.

Then he looked to my dad. "You sticking around?"

"I got to repair a dock at the Pelletier camp."

The Pelletier camp was on Sugar Island, one of the many nodules of land dotting the surface of the lake, like the specks on a brown trout. Each fall Dad repaired docks or did other odd jobs for some of the property owners who lived out of town.

Perry wiped off his hands with a rag. "Water could get choppy."

"That's a good thing," Dad said. "It'll keep it from freezing."

Then he grinned and put his arm around my shoulder. For some reason I remember the weight of it. "Give her a ride when you're finished, will ya?"

"You bet."

That was it. There wasn't some big exchange or something unusual like in the movies. For that still moment, my father was strong and smiling, his hair a little disheveled. It was a day like any other day. Only it wasn't like any other day.

I took off my jacket and gloves and hat. Hung everything up on the pegs by the door.

"Work late last night?" Perry asked.

"Dorrie sent me home around ten," I said. "Things got kind of slow."

Dorrie owned and ran the Lazy Moose, a restaurant and bar where I waited tables three nights a week.

Perry tossed me his rag. "How about you start under the car. Grease every fitting you can find."

I picked up the grease gun off one of the workbenches, then squatted toward the ground, lay back on the creeper, and pushed myself underneath the car. I wiped the old grease off each fitting and pumped new grease into it.

"When you finish, pull the drain plug out of the rear axle. I got some new ninety weight I'm going to replace it with."

That was how the morning went, Perry giving me directions. The two of us working on my car. He changed the spark plug wires, replaced the distributor with a new MSD electronic ignition. I bled the braking system and adjusted the rear brake shoes. Perry helped me replace the front brake pads.

Though it wasn't yet noon, the daylight through the windows dimmed. "(I Can't Get No) Satisfaction" faded in and out over the radio. Perry knew all the words and sang along. The wind was picking up, a wailing sound like somebody weeping.

"Gonna have us a doozy," Perry said.

I thought of my father for a second then. I wish it had been longer. Dad, in his six-seater Thompson. I didn't worry about him. I just pictured him for that second, specifically his hands, as if I could feel his muscles contracting from the cold, and I wondered what gloves he had worn.

Perry handed me a doughnut, which I ate lying down. Other than that, we worked until a little after one, not stopping for lunch.

"You gonna touch up the paint?" he asked me.

"Next weekend," I said.

"If I'm not around, your dad's got a key. You know where everything is."

Perry gave me a ride back to the house. Snow shot toward us like porcupine quills. The wipers slapped hard back and forth. I thought about what I would eat for lunch. Perhaps Perry was hungry too, as he said very little.

We pulled into the driveway, over a fifty-yard straight stretch of frozen snow and gravel, the consistency of peanut brittle.

"See ya, Little Bit."

"Later," I said.

The house was quiet, the dull afternoon light barely filtering in through the windows. Linda always cleaned the church on Saturdays. Brought the twins with her and let them play in one of the Sunday school rooms. Linda told us how sometimes they'd stand at the lectern to the right of the altar and pretend they were priests.

On the kitchen table was a note. *Mike, chili casserole in the fridge. Put in the oven around four. XXO.*

Linda was always leaving notes for my father on the fridge or on the bathroom mirror, sticky notes that either gave him things to do or told him how much she loved him. People said Linda was good to my dad. People like Perry and my grandmother, Mémère, Dad and Perry's mom. Linda cooked my dad's dinner, rubbed his back, poured his brandy. She liked to take care of the house. In other words, Linda didn't leave him. But other than cleaning the church, which she didn't get paid for, she didn't have a job outside of the home. I could understand her staying with the twins when they were younger. But Scott and Alex had been in school now for over three years. Maybe if Linda had held a job, Dad wouldn't have had to work so much. Maybe he wouldn't have been out on his boat repairing a dock on a snowy afternoon.

I looked at the clock on the stove. Almost one thirty. I made lunch. Maybe I ate tuna fish. Maybe roast beef. I don't remember. Yet I remember the crumbs on the counter that I wiped up with a damp rag. I remember setting my plate into the sink. I walked into the den and picked up a Stephen King book I'd been reading. *The Green Mile*.

I lay back against the arm of the sofa and read for about an hour. Then I looked through the window at the snow. Watched the thick hedge of white that fell from the sky and swirled in funnels across the lawn like dancing ghosts. I didn't think of my dad, which now makes me ache somewhere deep in my throat. I didn't think of anything. I just watched the snow.

The phone rang. I thought about getting up to answer it, but I didn't. Maybe I thought it was Dorrie and she'd ask me to work. Maybe I just didn't want to move. To this day, I wonder who called.

I slept, the blue throw Linda had crocheted pulled over my shoulders. When I awoke, the house was almost dark. Outside, the snow continued to fall, though gentler than before and barely visible against the shaded sky. I walked to the kitchen. The note was still on the table. The stove was cold. I slipped on my boots, left the house from the back door, stood in the driveway, and faced the road, the wind fighting my hair and stinging my hands. I felt a numbness in my stomach, felt it rise through my chest, felt my body stiffen. I dug my heels into the frozen ground and pivoted to my left. There I stood, watching the road that led to and from town, the snow striking silently, like floury ash.

CHAPTER

2

It was almost five thirty by the time Linda pulled into the driveway. I was standing in the kitchen, about to preheat the oven. My cell phone lay on the counter in front of me. I'd called my dad's number a half dozen times, each time getting his voice mail: "Hey, this is Mike. Leave a message." I'd left a couple of messages, but he hadn't called back. My coat hung by the back door. I was still wearing my boots, as if caught between worry and convincing myself that my dad was okay.

From the kitchen window, I watched the twins climb out each side of the blue Subaru wagon and run for the house, a cloud of snow and breath trailing behind them.

Dad had probably met up with Perry or stopped by the Lazy Moose. Perhaps he'd checked in with Linda.

The wiring on the garage door had shorted out some time ago—something Dad had said he was going to fix one of these days. Linda climbed out of the wagon and raised the door manually. I felt myself almost yell, "Stop!" or "Wait!" My father's truck wasn't there. I might need the car later to go out with friends; I might need it to look for him. Linda wouldn't have heard me yell anyway.

I didn't preheat the oven. A gust of air swathed my face as Alex and Scott entered the house. In the tumble of boots and layers that fell to the floor, I slipped on my own coat and hat and met Linda just outside the door. She was carrying a bag of groceries.

"Need a hand?" I asked.

"No, I got it. Where's Mike?"

She looked around briefly as if making sure his truck wasn't there, though she already knew it wasn't. "Has he been home yet?"

"I haven't seen him."

Linda ran her free hand over her head, peeling off her knit cap. She stared away, perhaps at the snow or the road or her own worry as flakes melted on her freckled skin.

"May I borrow the car?" I asked.

"In this weather? Where are you going?"

"I'll be fine. I'm just going to town."

"What about supper?"

"I already ate."

She handed me the keys, her hands reddened and chafed. It was the little things about Linda that bothered me—the fact that she had to vacuum the house every morning, that she pinched her lips together too tightly when she was thinking, that she would cut out coupons but she wouldn't work. And yet, I knew it was the fact that my dad loved her that annoyed me the most.

Linda stepped inside; I walked to the garage. I lifted the door and shoved it upward with both hands, then waited a couple of seconds to see if it would stay. I take after my mom—in height, in her lean build, and in the same dark eyes that cast shadows over her pallid skin.

I drove the two-mile stretch to town, the slick white covering over the frost heaves in the road like moguls on a ski slope. Hulking black shapes of spruce and fir towered on either side of me, then broken pastureland and occasional houses whose lights, resembling distant lanterns, dotted the surface. Something stung my stomach and burned its way upward. I'd felt it before, like a hole dead center in my belly. A fear as black as the night around me. I wondered when it would go away, close itself up like a scar. When things were good I barely noticed it. And life was good, wasn't it?

It wasn't the first time someone had gone looking for my dad. Once his snowmobile had gotten stuck. Another time he'd fallen asleep in his truck after a night at the bar. He hadn't been drunk. Just tired.

A vehicle drove toward me. I slowed as it passed, and recognized the tow truck that belonged to Annie's dad. Annie lived behind me about a half mile. We'd grown up together and considered ourselves best friends. I would give her a call later, once Dad was home. I would tell her about how worried he'd had everybody.

Annie's dad, like most of the other men in Sebaticuk, worked two jobs. That's what people did where we lived.

Money didn't come easy. Mr. Therriault was a welder during the day. He towed vehicles during the nights and weekends, like a doctor on call. My dad was a delimber during the week. In the spring and early summer when the mud set in, he stained decks and houses, mostly for property owners from out of town and a few of the local elderly. In the fall he spent his weekends repairing docks, cutting across the lake in the small Thompson he'd bought from Linda's dad.

Moosehead Lake is a reservoir for the Kennebec River. In the fall the Department of Inland Fisheries and Wildlife opens the floodgates on the lake's east outlet, releasing the overflow into the river, where it eventually empties into the ocean. The process prepares the lake for the spring runoff from the mountains and draws the lake's water level down a good five to six feet by late fall. November was the perfect time to repair docks, as the water was always at its lowest level. Dad had repaired docks for as far back as I could remember. He was a big man. He was strong. A steel giant that nothing could harm. Why was I afraid?

At the junction in town, I took a right on Highway 15 and drove north toward the inlet where Dad always put in his boat. The icy road carved upward over Scammon Ridge, my tires spinning out more than a time or two before the highway dipped down toward the isthmus between Prong Pond and Otter Cove. I turned left into the small parking area near the boat ramp. Within seconds the beam from my headlights caught the reflectors from the trailer that was hitched to my dad's truck. Something thick like oil drenched my breath, a knowing that he was out there, somewhere, unless his truck wouldn't start, unless he'd picked up a ride from someone, or maybe when the snow had blown in he'd holed up at the camp.

I left the car running, kept the lights on, their cone-shaped glow fanning out over the lake in front of me. I couldn't get out of the car fast enough, banging my shin on the bottom edge of the door, wanting to fly to my dad's truck, my legs, my lungs, my fingers, nothing moving fast enough to get me there, as if the desperate momentum of my body and the tangible evidence of his truck would make him materialize. Where the hell was he?

I reached his truck, both hands on the cold exterior. I pulled at the handle, gripping it with everything I had, throwing the weight of my body into each heaving lug. The windshield, the windows, even the metal was frosted over, everything damp and cold and icy. And the door, too, was frozen. I blew air on the handle, exhaled until I became dizzy, all the while continuing to work the lever. Finally it released. I climbed into the truck, the vinyl seats as cold as the flesh of fish on ice. I looked around the truck for some sign, some message. The keys lay on the floorboard where Dad always left them. My hands shook as I inserted the starter key into the ignition. The engine turned over. I gave it gas; it kicked in smoothly, and I swore, names and words I cannot remember. He hadn't made it back to his truck. He was out there. I turned on the lights, switched on the high beams, their rays combining with the headlights from Linda's wagon, reaching maybe two hundred yards over the lake, reflecting off the flakes of snow sifting and swirling through the air. The wind blew in off the lake in steady gusts. Even inside the truck I could feel its drafts, hear the waves as they crashed against the pitched shoreline that climbed its way toward buttresses of shale and thick patches of spruce and hemlock.

"Steady, Gen," Mike used to tell me when I'd race. "You're the commander." And so, after shutting everything off, I commanded my legs, my body out of the truck and walked to the wagon. I backed out onto the road and turned toward town, cursing myself for having left my cell phone at the house. I tried to conjure up reasons for why my dad hadn't returned to his truck, but none of them, including him hunkering down at the Pelletier camp for the night because his boat wouldn't start or because the winds had been too strong, could quiet the thrust of blood pulsing in my head. Ever since my mom had left, my father was all I really had. Linda was Scott and Alex's mom. She was my dad's wife. She was another woman in the house. She wasn't mine in the sense that she didn't belong to me. My dad did, and nothing I told myself could squelch my fear that the person who loved me most might not be coming home.

And then the feeling of "this isn't really happening." Yet, I knew it *could* happen. It *did* happen, at least once or twice a year. Last March, Christine Bédard had met a group of friends at the water's edge near Burnt Jacket Mountain. She was home from college. Everyone knows the ice there is soft. There's too much turbulence under the surface. She wasn't thinking, or perhaps she'd had too much to drink. Decided to do crazy eights over the lake. The back of her car broke the ice first. Her friends could only stand on the bank and watch. Within a half hour, Search and Rescue from the Department of Inland Fisheries and Wildlife pulled her car out. The water wasn't much more than twenty feet deep. But even if they had pulled the car out within five minutes, or even two, it wouldn't have mattered. Once the lake's temperature drops to thirty-two degrees, it takes only thirty seconds for a person's heart to stop.

It was sometime in January that a couple of out-of-town snowmobilers and their machines went down off Seboomook Point. Hazard signs had been posted, but the snowfall was so dense, the signs, no doubt, had been invisible to the drivers, who weren't familiar with the precarious stretches of ice floe.

Just on the east edge of town was the police department. I turned into the parking area, the frozen surface grinding beneath my tires. I had been there only once before, on a field trip in second grade. I couldn't believe

I was doing this, that I was there, about to tell a police officer that my dad was missing.

I shut off the engine and climbed out of the car. There it was again—the wind and snow and an emptiness I couldn't name. I wanted to scream just to fill the god-awful space.

"Hang on, Dad. I'm coming for you. You're going to be okay." I think I actually said those words, kept saying them with the quiet intensity of a pleading prayer.

The office for the police department was in a small, one-story brick building. The radiators alongside the wall made a steady drone. The air was too warm and dry. I could feel the perspiration from my scalp trapped beneath my hat, could smell the damp wool. In front of me was a large desk behind which the dispatcher sat reading a paperback. Nellie Dupris had been the dispatcher most of my life, but she had retired the year before. This girl was new, maybe in her twenties, and not someone I had seen around town. She held up a finger when I walked in as if wanting to finish the last paragraph she was reading.

"My dad is missing," I said.

That was the first time she looked up, the first time I noticed something was wrong with her. Her left eye was too large, at least twice the size of her right eye, making her entire face appear crooked. Her hair was stringy and dirty blond. She turned the book over, setting it on the desk, then picked up a pen.

"I didn't have my cell phone, or I would have called nine-one-one," I told her.

"What's his name?" she asked.

Her eyes were blue, her left eye like a lens on a scope, giving me the uneasy feeling that she could see too much.

"Mike Sommer."

"Do you know the point of his last location?"

"Otter Cove, at the public boat launch. He was supposed to be fixing a dock at a camp on Sugar Island."

I didn't have to say anything else. Officer Whalen appeared from a hallway behind the desk. "The sheriff's already been dispatched," he said. "He's putting a call through to the warden."

I didn't understand.

Officer Whalen walked around the desk and laid a hand on my shoulder. "Linda called," he said. "About five minutes ago. She also said to keep a lookout for you."

The sheriff's office was in Dover-Foxcroft, about an hour's drive southeast of town. Search and Rescue typically consisted of a type of triage. A missing person would be reported either directly to the sheriff's office or to the police, who would then dispatch the sheriff. If the person was missing somewhere in the forests or on one of the lakes, the sheriff would contact the warden on call with the Department of Inland Fisheries and Wildlife. With the help of other law enforcement, the IFW would organize a search. I knew the protocol. I'm sure everyone in our parts did.

"His truck's at the boat launch," I told Officer Whalen.

I'd known Officer Whalen most all of my life, saw him at church from time to time or riding around on his motorcycle in the summer. He had blond hair that was beginning to gray and a lean build that had turned soft in the middle. He knew the difference between teenagers having fun and teenagers putting themselves in danger, and he wrote his tickets accordingly. The right corner of his mouth would twitch slowly upward every so often, in a wink of a grin, as if giving his onlooker an approving gesture. He was kind and carried a long-suffering smile, almost hidden by his bushy mustache, as if he felt sorry for the whole wide world and understood a hell of a lot more than he cared to.

"I want to talk to the warden," I said.

Officer Whalen pulled a cigarette out of his shirt pocket, tapped it on the desk at least five or six times, all the while staring down at it. Then, ever so methodically, he placed it between his lips and lit it with a lighter he'd taken out of the side pocket of his trousers. He drew deeply on the tobacco. With his thumb and index finger, he pinched hold of the cigarette, lowered it to his side, and exhaled with just as much slow deliberation.

"I think Gormley's on call tonight," he said. "Should be at the cove about now. I'll drive you over."

"That's okay. I've got a car."

I proceeded outside to my car, with Officer Whalen right behind me.

"I'm parked around back," he said. "Go ahead. I'll meet you there."

Officer Whalen's cigarette smoke had trailed into my vehicle like a spirit. I was glad for its presence, as if the bulk of fear congesting every ounce of my blood didn't have to be carried by me alone. There would be others now, and I had to believe those others would bring my father home.

CHAPTER

3

Seeing my father's empty truck and trailer again against the black expanse of the lake and sky intensified my fear. He was still out there. I pulled in next to a white Ford pickup. A woman holding a flashlight was standing next to my dad's vehicle. Immediately I was disappointed, believing only a man as big and strong as my dad could have any chance of finding him.

No sooner did I climb out of the wagon, than Officer Whalen drove up beside me. I waited for him before approaching the warden. Snow continued to sift and swirl, as the wind stirred in steady gusts, maybe about twenty knots, though not quite as aggressive as earlier in the day.

Officer Whalen pressed his palm against my back. The two of us walked toward the warden.

"Kathy, this is Mike's daughter," Officer Whalen said.

Kathy shook my gloved hand.

The distance and her long hair had deceived me. She looked as strong as any man. She had to be close to six feet, with heft to her bones. Her hair was black and straight and hung halfway down her back. Her legs looked long and sturdy. Her face had the broad cheekbones and angular contours of some of the Algonquin I had known, and her raven eyes, almond shaped and deep set, glistened in the glow from her flashlight, now pointed toward the ground.

"I'm Genesis," I told her.

She stood at least a foot taller than me. For a moment, I had the sensation that I was kneeling in her presence.

"We get calls like this all the time," the warden said. "Someone forgot to check in at home, or decided to take off with a friend."

"But his truck's here," I reminded her.

"Maybe his boat wouldn't start. He could have gotten a ride with someone. At least a half-dozen crafts were out on the water today. The way this storm blew in, I'm sure he had enough mind to stay put at the camp."

I'd told myself all the same things.

"There's not a whole lot we can do right now," she went on. "We can't take a boat out in this weather. Even if the winds ease up close to shore, the waves can kick up three to five feet once you're a hundred yards out. By morning we can get a helicopter or an airboat on search. If he's not at the Pelletier camp, he could have had motor trouble, used his oars and camped out at one of the other cabins."

"There's probably a hundred islands out there with some sort of shelter," Officer Whalen said. "I guarantee you he's safe and dry."

"Did he have his cell phone with him?" Kathy asked me.

"I tried calling it earlier. The phone was on, but he didn't answer."

The warden was wearing leather gloves. She opened my father's truck door, touching as little space on the handle as possible. It opened more easily this time. She knelt on the seat and looked around—on the floorboards, in the back of the cab—occasionally moving some of the clutter—an old sweatshirt of my dad's, a toolbox. She looked inside the toolbox as well.

Her jacket, dark green, hung down over her hips. She lifted one side of it and reached for her cell phone from her belt clip. "What's your dad's number?"

I gave it and she punched in the numbers. I knew she was checking to see if the phone was in the truck. Unless the battery had gone dead, the phone wasn't there.

"We're going to have to impound the vehicle." She climbed out and stood beside me.

"Why?"

"It's just standard procedure," Officer Whalen told me.

They would be taking my dad's truck to the impound lot, an acre-size piece of land surrounded by an eight-foot-tall chain-link fence with barbed wire angled in from the top. Some of the vehicles were sheltered by metal housing, much like a carport. Vehicles that had already been autopsied remained in the open. The lot contained a handful of vehicles at any given time. The only car I'd ever recognized there had belonged to M. J. Mahoney, who'd disappeared almost a year after returning home from the war in Iraq. His right arm had been shattered in a bombing. I'd waited on him at the Lazy Moose. Watched him eat with his left hand. He was twenty-four and his Mercury Cougar was just about the same age, the once smooth vinyl roofing having turned the texture of both rawhide and lichen, and the maroon body faded to a lavender-pink. On the way home from school one day, my friend Annie and I had watched the police do a search of the vehicle. They sectioned off parts of the car with a large piece of clear plastic while they pressed fingerprint tape to every inch of the car's surface. Finally, Annie and I got bored and drove on. Two weeks later a couple of hunters found Mahoney's body in the woods with a gunshot wound to the head and a .357 magnum in his left hand. Last I'd looked, the car was still at the impound lot, and for the first time, I wondered why.

"How early can you get a pilot out?" I asked.

"If the snow clears, as early as daybreak," Kathy told me. "We'll have an incident command team organized by morning in case he doesn't show up tonight."

"What about in the meantime?" My dad was out there

somewhere, cold, hungry, and we were going to let hours pass by without doing a damn thing.

"Someone will be out to the house to talk to your family. Other than that, just pray for a clearing."

Did Kathy believe in God? Would she be praying, too?

"I'll follow you back to the house," Officer Whalen said. "Stay with you and your family till a warden gets there."

At that moment, I had the strangest feeling, as if it wasn't my father out there, but someone else we were looking for—a cousin, or Perry, or one of my father's friends, and that when I got home, Dad would be there, sitting at the kitchen table with Linda, rubbing her back like he would do and drinking a beer or coffee while we all waited for daybreak and for the snow to clear.

"Gen?" Officer Whalen asked tentatively. "You okay?"

I didn't answer him right away. I was standing there perplexed because I couldn't decide whether my dad would be drinking beer or coffee on a night when someone was missing and the whole family was worried, and I wanted to know, didn't want to move until I'd figured it out.

I looked out over the lake, licked the droplets of melted snow off my upper lip. That's when it hit me—the night my father had come home and found out my mom wasn't there. I was only six, and yet the image was

suddenly as clear as the mountains on a spring morning—
the smell of his breath as he held me to him with one
arm, the coffee mug he supported on his left knee, the
rise and fall of his chest as we stared out the window.

"She'll come back," Perry had told him. But she never
did.

CHAPTER
4

Almost five hours had passed since I'd spoken with Warden Gormley. My father still wasn't home. I was sitting
at the kitchen table. Linda was to my left. My grandmother, Mémère, my dad's mom, who lived about a mile
from our house, was to my right, and directly across
from me was a man by the name of Frank. He was a large
man with a reddish face, who worked for the Inland
Waters Search and Rescue. He said he had gone to school
with my dad and that he lived in Rockport now. He'd
brought his dog, a black Labrador he called Henry. The
dog was lying by my feet.

Perry had not come by the house yet, and I wondered
if he was out looking for his brother, despite the weather
conditions. Perry and Mike had always been close, three
years apart in age, with Perry the older.

Linda had made coffee. We each held a cup. The man
by the name of Frank had brought sandwiches, which
remained in a bag on the counter, untouched. He'd been

designated to look after the family, to be the middle man between us and the incident command team.

"The incident lieutenant and some of the volunteers will be setting up a command post at the boat launch," Frank told us.

"When?" Mémère asked.

"In the morning. They'll be bringing over a motor home." He paused before continuing. "You won't be allowed to help with the search and rescue. You'd be a liability. We'll want you at the post site though."

Mémère leaned over the table. "What do you mean, we can't help with the search?" She spoke in a heavy, French-Canadian accent that thickened when she was under stress. She and my grandfather had lived in New Brunswick until just before my dad was born, forty-five years ago, before my grandfather came south to take a job as a logger. My grandmother, sixty-five, didn't look a day over fifty, and her body moved with the force and efficiency of someone half her age. She had short, unruly red hair that she'd long ago given up taming, copper skin, and green eyes. She'd lost my grandfather when my dad was nineteen. Three years later she married a man named Harry, who worked at a mill in Bangor and traveled home on the weekends.

"I'll stay with you the whole time," Frank said. "You'll hear everything that's going on."

"*Pshh.*" Mémère pushed herself back against her chair.

{ 30 }

"You'll help by being there," Frank told her. "We need you."

Frank wrapped his hands around the cup in front of him, his fingers interlocking. "You and Linda and Genesis know Mike better than anyone. You *have* to stay at the command post. There are going to be questions. Things we didn't think of earlier. What if we spot a red coat, only you told us he was wearing something brown. Does he own a red coat, for example? Maybe he grabbed one from the back of his truck before he headed out. Maybe kept one on his boat."

"He doesn't own a red coat," Linda said.

"You see, that's what I'm talking about." Frank scooted his chair back several inches from the table, like someone who had just finished a large meal. "We don't know that sort of information unless we talk with you."

"But you said he's probably holed up in one of the camps," I told him. "If that's the case, then what difference would it make if he's wearing a green coat or a red coat?"

"It could matter, if the pilot spots him outside one of the cabins."

"*Oh, mon Dieu.*" Mémère shook her head.

"There'll be a pilot going out in the morning?" Linda asked.

"Randy Haycock. He's been doing search and rescue for thirty-some years. Lives down in Dover-Foxcroft. He's the lieutenant's right-hand man. As long as the weather's clear, he'll fly. He's taken his helicopter out in forty-knot winds before. That's never stopped him. He just has to be able to see. Visibility is the key."

Frank continued, "The whole place will be in action as early as four or five, setting up the command post, clearing a landing pad."

"As long as the weather breaks," I said.

Frank nodded stiffly. "We have to get a break in the weather." He looked down at his coffee cup, which no doubt was empty by now. "We're doing everything we can. We can't risk one of our own. Not at a time like this. That does us no good."

"How are you doing everything you can? What does that mean?" Linda asked.

Frank hesitated before answering, as if carefully gauging his words. "Over half of the protocol measures have already been taken. Search and rescue teams have been organized. The pilot's ready to take off early in the morning from the sheriff's helipad. Divers have been called. They'll be on standby at the command post."

It was that last piece of information that he'd been afraid to tell us. He didn't need to say anything more. Only thirty seconds in the water and my dad would be dead. Anywhere from eight to twelve hours had passed from the time he should have been home. In water like Moosehead Lake, this late in the year, divers recovered bodies; they didn't rescue lives.

"I'll make some fresh coffee," Mémère said, because

she needed to do something, or because what remained in the bottom of the carafe was thickening like tar. I couldn't decide. Funny, why these things mattered to me. I wanted to know the reason for everything, like why this man was here drinking coffee at our table. Did he have a wife and kids of his own to go home to? And why had the twins fallen asleep on the sofa—why had at least one of them not crawled into bed down the hall?

The clock on the stove was digital. Twelve forty-seven. I stared at it waiting for the next number to appear. Twelve forty-eight, then twelve forty-nine.

CHAPTER
5

I stood up from the table and walked into the den. No one seemed to notice me leave except the dog, who raised his head for a brief moment before resting it again on his paws. Alex was curled up on one end of the sofa. Scott was lying on his back on the other end, with his legs sprawled out to the sides. The blue throw I had used earlier in the day lay in a wad between them, no doubt kicked from their bodies in their deep sleep. I shook out the throw, draped it on top of them, and tucked it over each of their shoulders, first Alex, then Scott. They smelled differently. I had never noticed that before. Alex had the smell of salty skin and fresh air, like a boy who's just come in from playing hard outdoors. Scott smelled of bed sheets, and his hair had the faint odor of rumpled pajamas that have been worn too long.

I sat on the floor, facing the sofa, holding my knees to my chest, watching my half brothers. Even through the downiness of their sleep, there was a luster to their skin, a playful glow beneath the fawn-colored freckles that spanned the bridge of their noses and swept beneath their eyes. Their freckles looked exactly the same, as if the sun had splayed its rays upon them equally. How could that be? Wisps of brown hair scooped over their foreheads. My dad would have said they needed a haircut, but Linda loved it when their hair grew over their ears and slightly down their necks.

They seemed small as I watched them sleep—younger and more vulnerable than I'd been at that age. They were seven, just about the same age I'd been when I started racing snowmobiles, about a year after my mom had left. But the twins had always had a mom. Maybe that's what made them seem younger. I'd had two years where my world had centered solely around my father and me.

Alex stirred but didn't wake. They should start racing, I thought. I should get them on their own machines. Dad will have to take them, I was quick to tell myself, when he gets back.

Snowmobile season would begin soon, not long after Thanksgiving if there was enough snow. And then the realization that Thanksgiving was a week away, and after that, Christmas. Fear rose up in my throat like bile. I swallowed hard to push it away, a battle that was becoming exhausting.

The first Christmas after my mom left, Dad didn't even put up a tree. I'd wrapped tiny strips of tin foil around the branches of a ficus plant that my mom had left behind. I'd watered the plant faithfully, even talked to it, to keep it alive, as if maintaining a piece of my mother's presence. Dad and I were supposed to have Christmas dinner at Mémère's. As we were getting on our coats to leave, Perry pulled up to the house with a Mini Z Ski-Doo snowmobile on a trailer behind his truck. "Merry Christmas," Dad said, with the kind of grin on his face that let me know from then on everything was going to be okay, or at least he was going to do his damnedest to make sure things got better.

A couple of weeks later I ran my first drag at Caratunk, along the Kennebec River. I placed third out of fifteen other sleds. Dad stood proudly at the finish line, bundled up in his parka and Russian ushanka, the earflaps of that big fur hat flailing in the air as he jumped up and down.

After that first race, I was hooked. I'd speed back and forth along the driveway of our home, a two-story farmhouse a couple of miles east of town. On the weekends, Dad and I traveled what's called the circuit, where I ran both oval and drag for the next five years, even after Linda came into our lives and the twins were born.

But the traveling grew tiresome. One weekend we'd be in Skowhegan, the next in Lewiston, and sometimes we'd travel to the Mahoosuc Range in New Hampshire or toward the east just outside of New Brunswick.

And then there was the year the snow didn't come, not in the abundance we were used to, anyway. The skies remained mostly clear. Instead of two and three feet of accumulation and drifts as high as rooftops, the ground bore only a residue of the white stuff, which amounted to nothing more than four to six inches, just enough to freeze over and turn to ice, not the kind of packing snow that a snowmobile can tread on. That didn't stop the temperatures from dropping though. In fact, records show that season was one of Maine's coldest, the lake freezing to three feet deep, clear plastic duct-taped to every home's windows.

I was twelve then. One night in January, just after dark, I had come inside from playing Lost in the Wilderness with Annie. I know that makes me sound young—playing games like that at twelve—but it's true. If I wasn't riding my sled, I was building forts or pretending I had to scrounge around for food.

"Gen, I've been thinking," Dad said.

My father was sitting on the sofa in front of the pellet stove, his body sunken into the cushions as if he was all banked in for the night. He had his feet up on the coffee table. He was always thinking, even when he was drinking a beer and playing pool at Woody's or watching a football game with his friends. There was this kind of distance to him, something wistful, like he could be in his head and talk at the same time.

"You know the racing association on the west side of the lake?" he said.

I pulled off my boots and my jacket and walked over to the sofa, where I sat beside him.

"They're starting a youth league," he told me.

"They're going to let kids race?" I asked.

"Yep."

The association he was referring to was the West Cove Ice Racing Association. The group had been organized a few years back. Each year since it began, as soon as the lake would freeze two feet deep, the group would hold races at Wharf Junction, on the opposite side of the lake from Sebaticuk. They'd plow a wide, quarter-mile track about a half mile out over the water. I'd seen a couple of the races, probably the only two times I hadn't had a sled competition on the same day. Locals would pick up junkers around town, then modify them to meet the racing specs.

"So I've been thinking," he said again. "It doesn't look like there's going to be a lot of sled races on the docket this year, with the weather and all."

I crossed my feet next to his and listened, hopeful.

"Maybe we ought to switch gears," he said. "What about us staying around here on the weekends and you racing cars instead of a sled? We wouldn't have to be counting on the snow. Just the ice."

Funny, now, looking back. We can always count on there being ice. Sometimes not as early as November, but eventually it happens. The lake freezes over, turns into one enormous palette of white.

I told my dad, of course I wanted to race cars. I was only twelve, so I asked him how I would reach the gas pedal and the brake. He told me we'd strap blocks onto the pedals, and that's what we did. I started racing with a 1991 Subaru Legacy that Mike picked up from Perry. When I turned sixteen, Perry found the '93 Mustang at a trade auction in Lewiston. That was the year I entered the adult rear-wheel division, which I'd been racing in ever since.

I thought again of the twins, tried to remember if they'd even driven a snowmobile by themselves. I was sure they hadn't. I wondered if my racing had gotten in the way.

The backdoor opened, releasing a breath of cold air that traveled across the kitchen and into the den.

I looked up to see Perry through the doorway. He nodded in my direction. His face was as grim as I was feeling, his cheeks dour and wet from the snow, his eyes tired creases.

"You been out there?" asked Mémère. "*Mere de Dieu!* If I don't have to be worrying about you, too."

"Just along the shorelines," Perry said. "The wind's kicking the bow back in my face. Snow's still coming down."

My own paralysis felt toxic. Perry had at least tried. It wasn't the darkness that locked us in. The pilot could wear night-vision goggles. It was the snow. "Poor visibility," Frank had called it. And even though there was only a slim chance that the wind could hold the pilot back, it certainly kept any boats from making a dent in the search. It was this harsh, unforgiving place we called home that was controlling our lives, and for the most part always had.

I looked back at the twins, leaned my head against the arm cushion of the sofa.

"Want some coffee?" Linda asked Perry.

"No thanks."

"I'm Frank." Chair legs shifted against the floor as the introduction was made.

The exchange of voices continued, eventually settling like a drunken sleep that seemed to leak itself into my own veins, as if we were all connected. My back was to the kitchen. I didn't hear Perry approach. It was his hand over my head that first startled me. He sat on the floor next to me, pulled his own legs up to his chest, as if helping me watch over the boys.

"They look so peaceful." His deep voice, soft and steady and not much more than a whisper, carved something comfortable into the silence.

"You didn't see anything?" I asked.

"No." Perry wrapped his arm around my shoulder and pulled me to him. "Little Bit?"

"Yeah?"

"There's patches of fog. Snow and fog like thick soup. I could barely see my hand in front of me."

My body stiffened. Perry must have felt it. "Don't beat yourself up. There's nothing you, or I, or anyone else can do right now. Your dad's a smart man. Don't forget that."

"Then why am I so afraid? Why do I miss him as if he's already gone?"

"That's what you do when you love someone."

"It's torture," I said.

Perry held me tighter. "Yes, it is."

"Goddamn the fog," I said. "And the wind and the snow."

I looked up toward the window to check the weather, but all I could see in the black glass was the reflection of the room. If the fog lingered till morning, it would slow the air search, not to mention the lake could freeze. As indigenous to northern Maine as the wind and snow and cold is the fog, the kind of thick vapor that settles around the trees, the land, and one's skin like a spirit, a stillness that slows everything, including the water's currents. The water was already cold enough, at least thirty degrees. Once the currents slowed, the lake's entire surface could turn to one enormous sheet of ice. And then an image flashed in my mind—my dad swimming, flailing his arms toward a ceiling too thick for him to break through.

CHAPTER
6

It must have been two in the morning by the time Perry and Frank left. Linda and Mémère had turned in, my grandmother having decided to sleep in the extra bedroom off of the living room. I was in my bed upstairs, the covers pulled up to my chin, as if tucking myself into a cocoon. I reached for the phone to call Annie.

"Do you want me to come over?" she asked, after I'd told her about Dad.

"No. I'm going to try and get some sleep." I was lying on my back, staring into a poster of stars that, years before, I'd thumbtacked to the ceiling.

"I'm sure he's okay," Annie said.

"I know. That's what I keep telling myself." I turned onto my side, pulling the covers over my shoulder. "What did you do today?" I asked.

"Gina had to work, so I watched her kids. The baby cried a lot. The rest of the day, Andrew and I played video games."

Gina was Annie's sister. She waited tables at the

Boom Chain, a locals' favorite that served breakfast and lunch.

I listened to my friend until I began to drift off to sleep. Listening to something ordinary was medicinal. The last time I'd laid on my bed, I, too, had known an ordinary life.

. . .

By morning, the snow had stopped, leaving maybe eight inches of accumulation in the low spots, and I'm sure over a foot in the surrounding mountains. I'd slept a couple of hours, but by four o'clock was wide awake, with a nervous pounding in my head. I dressed and hurried downstairs. A light was on in the kitchen. Linda and Mémère were talking in soft, measured voices. The twins were still asleep on the sofa. Linda had decided that she and I would drive to the boat launch. Mémère would stay back at the house to watch over Scott and Alex. Sounds are louder in the early morning. I had never noticed that before—the way each footstep in the snow, the garage door as it lifted in its tracks, the turning over of the car engine was crisper and more distinct.

The sky appeared fair, brightened by a crescent moon and a spattering of stars. "It's clear," I said, the only two words I'd spoken since we'd left the house.

"That may not be a good thing."

I looked at Linda; her gloved hands gripped the top of the steering wheel. "What do you mean?"

"If it was clear, he'd be home. He'd have found his way back." Her voice was matter-of-fact and so even it frightened me, as if she knew something the rest of us didn't.

"Not if he'd had boat trouble," I told her. "Or maybe he's still asleep at one of the camps." I was defensive but tried to sound calm.

As we drove closer to the lake, however, the weather changed. Though the winds remained still and the sky free of precipitation, the air was thickening, which was often the case over the lake and shore. As we approached Scammon Ridge, the fog banks had become so dense we could barely see ten feet in front of us.

Linda leaned forward as she strained to see. "Damn!" She slammed both her hands onto the steering wheel.

"What's wrong?"

"I can't see. I can't see a fucking thing!" She was crying. Her breath struggled out of her, mixed with eerie, raspy moans, like she was trying to keep something big and monstrous inside, and she was losing the battle.

I didn't like Linda crying. I didn't know what to do with it. Once again, I felt like Linda was thinking the worst, and by thinking the worst, her very thoughts might keep my father away.

"Do you want me to drive?" I asked, because I didn't know what else to do.

She didn't answer. She just kept crying, never taking her hands off the steering wheel to wipe the dampness from her face.

{ 44 }

It was barely four thirty when we arrived at the boat launch. A man with a flashlight pointed us away from the parking lot, where a landing pad had been cleared. I immediately spotted the motor home. A covey of vehicles and headlights were scattered about. Linda pulled off to the side of the road about a hundred feet from the parking area. Frank was approaching us, carrying a cup in each hand. A shadow trailed behind him, which I assumed to be his dog. I was right.

As we got out of the car, Henry pressed himself against my leg and lifted his head for a pat, exhaling warm breath like puffs of smoke. Frank offered us coffee. Linda declined. I welcomed the warm liquid and caffeine.

"Did you manage any sleep?" Frank asked.

We began walking with him toward the motor home.

"Some," Linda said.

At the command station, a group of people in thick parkas gathered together just outside the door. The steam from their coffee quickly blended into the fog, making everything appear like one big, ominous apparition.

"Will the pilot be able to fly?" I asked.

Frank looked out over the lake, no doubt surveying the conditions. "It'll lift," he said. "The pilot's at the sheriff's station now, just waiting for the okay."

The sheriff's office was no more than twenty minutes by helicopter.

Frank placed his hand on Linda's shoulder, steering

her in the direction of a man walking toward us. "I want you to meet someone," he said.

The man was wearing a navy parka with some type of official patch sewn onto the left sleeve, and a fur bomber hat, reminding me of the Russian ushanka my dad would wear at my races.

"Linda and Genesis, this is Lieutenant Maynard," Frank said.

The man shook our hands. He wore brown leather gloves. His hands were large—too large for his medium-size frame. I guessed him to be around five ten, no taller than Perry.

"Lieutenant Maynard is the team commander," Frank went on to tell us.

The lieutenant had watery blue eyes and a broad, fleshy face. "You must be the family." His eyes had rested on me, though he was speaking to Linda as well.

"This is Mike's wife and daughter," Frank told him.

Lieutenant Maynard smiled, his lips pressed together, the creases in his face accordion-like. "Why don't we step inside the command station. It's a little warmer in there."

Frank and Henry waited outside while Linda and I followed the lieutenant into the mobile home. It felt roomy. Hot air from the propane heater blew out of the vents in the paneled walls. There was a table just to the right of the door with cushioned benches on either side. A long counter with a transmitter radio and a computer was at the other end of the room. A handful of people stood around the radio, some of them reading over papers they were holding.

Lieutenant Maynard motioned us to sit down at the table. I scooted in first. Linda sat next to me.

The lieutenant was now sitting across from us. He removed his large gloves and his hat, which he set on the seat beside him, and took out a small pad of paper and a pen from one of his coat pockets. He was balding, the crown of his head smooth and shiny beneath the light of the motor home. The rest of his hair was brown and thick and stood slightly on end from static electricity. I was focused more on his hair than on what he was saying. In fact, I wasn't even exactly sure what he was telling us. Something about being glad to meet us. Something about being sorry. Polite words that carried no substance. I was certain he said them to every family like ours that he met—families that had lost someone. And then I thought about the word *lost* and the word *found*. The two always went together, didn't they?

Linda nudged me. She and the lieutenant were looking at me.

"Who was the last person with Mike?" he asked, no doubt repeating his question.

"That would be me," I said. "And my uncle Perry."

"Around what time was that?"

I took off the wool hat my dad had given me, the one with long braids down the sides, and smoothed my hair. "It was in the morning. Around nine thirty, maybe, or a little before. My dad had taken me over to the garage where my uncle Perry works."

"Do you remember what your dad was wearing?" Lieutenant Maynard asked.

"He had on jeans," I said. My father appeared in my mind so clearly, as if he were still sitting next to me in the truck. The fabric of his jeans had become faded and polished at the knees—something I'd noticed when he'd pressed in the clutch, then slowly released it. I had thought that his legs looked strong, and had considered how small I was compared to him.

"What else?" the lieutenant asked.

"He has a brown slicker he wears over a fleece jacket when he takes the boat out, especially when it's snowing or wet. The fleece jacket is black. The slicker is like a windbreaker shell, only it has a hood." Words began escaping my mouth in a steady cadence, as if someone had turned on the switch of a battery-operated device inside me that controlled my speaking. "He was wearing the slicker," I said. "It smelled of fish and diesel oil. I almost told him to wash it, but we got talking about other things."

"When was that? What other things?" the lieutenant said.

"In the truck, on the way to the garage. We got talking about my car and the new differential Perry was going to install."

"She races cars," Linda told him. "On the ice."

The lieutenant nodded his head. He stared at his notes, all the while running his thumb back and forth over the pad of paper.

"Did you notice anything unusual about your dad?" he asked. "Anything out of the ordinary?"

"No." I pictured my father watching me as I spoke, making sure I was holding it together, making sure I didn't forget anything that needed to be said.

"Can you think of anything else I should know?" the lieutenant asked.

I looked into his eyes. They were so blue. Baptismal. And I wanted to say, "Bring him back to life," as if the lieutenant were God himself. What I meant was "our life." Bring him back to the way things had been. I thought of my dad swimming in a baptistery, trying to break to the surface. Perhaps I was remembering the flash I'd experienced the night before, an image that felt more like a dream from a deep sleep.

"There were life jackets on the boat," I told the lieutenant. "They were bright yellow, covered with white mesh. He never wore one, but he'd always get one out before he started the boat. He'd keep it on the floor near his feet. He has a seat cushion on the boat, too. It's orange."

Maybe the things I told the lieutenant didn't matter. He wrote them down anyway. What else did he want to know about my dad? How could I sum up his life, his habits, in just a few moments?

"His father died of a heart attack," Linda said, her face now composed. "When Mike was just nineteen."

Lieutenant Maynard was now looking at Linda dead-on.

I knew my grandfather had died of a heart attack when my dad was young, but what was Linda saying? That there were other risks I hadn't considered? Did my dad have a bad heart? Had he inherited some flaw from his dad? I never even knew my grandfather, but I had seen pictures. He didn't look like my dad. He looked small and fragile, someone Mémère could have run over just by the force of her laugh. I always thought my dad took after his mom. Mémère didn't have a bad heart, at least not that I knew of.

The door to the motor home opened. Frank poked his head in. "Genesis, there's someone here to see you."

As I stepped outside, Annie grabbed me in a hug with all of her broad, five-foot-eight-inch body.

"How did you know where to find me?" I asked, feeling huge relief that she'd come.

"Dad picked up the search on his scanner this morning. He drove me over."

Her light brown hair was still wet from her shower and pulled back in a ponytail, like she always wore it. She smelled of sweet shampoo and soap.

"Thanks for being here," I said.

I pulled away, looking around. Within the time I had been with the lieutenant, at least twenty more people had shown up. It was then that I realized the fog was thinning, allowing me to distinguish faces. I spotted Officer Whalen with a couple of the volunteers. More headlights threaded through the blackness toward the command post. Search teams had already been organized. In addition to the air search, people would be heading out on boats as soon as the lieutenant gave the okay. The way the sky was clearing, it wouldn't be long.

"Where's your dad now?" I asked Annie.

"He's meeting your uncle over at the Junction. They're taking Perry's boat out. They're going to brush the shores around the lake. See if they can spot anything from there."

Frank had told us we'd have to stay at the command station. Only those trained in search and rescue could assist with the actual search. Perry wasn't trained in search and rescue. I wished that he and Annie's dad were taking me with them.

"My muscles are going to atrophy if I don't do something soon," I said.

"I don't think it's going to be long before they find him," Annie said.

"What makes you say that?" I wanted her to keep talking. I wanted to believe in any fragment of hope. If someone had told me Santa Claus would be bringing my father home at midnight, I would have been sitting on my rooftop waiting.

"That's what my dad says. He thinks your dad had

motor trouble. That he's probably just floating, waiting for someone to pick him up."

"He didn't answer his cell phone," I told her.

"You can't always get a signal out on the lake. Especially around Kineo and some of the cliffs."

Kineo is a 150-acre peninsula of land extending from the easterly shore into the lake. It might as well be an island, connected to the mainland by only a narrow isthmus that at times is impassable, especially during the spring runoff. On the northernmost point of Kineo, climbs a seven-hundred-foot mountain, a large mass of hornstone rock allowing a nearly twenty-mile view of the lake in all directions. The mountain literally appears to rise out of the water like a Greek god.

I shoved my hands into my pockets, flexed my knees in and out to recover some warmth. Why hadn't I worn thermals or snow pants? I'd dressed in a hurry, grabbing a pair of jeans, which were now stiffening from the cold. The fog may have been lifting, but the temperature certainly wasn't. I looked to my friend. "Hey, Annie?"

"Yeah?"

"When a person gets cold, the heart works harder, right?"

"I suppose. What are you saying?"

"My grandfather died of a heart attack," I told her. "He wasn't very old. Somewhere in his forties. My dad's in his forties. Maybe Dad got really cold. Maybe his heart stopped working."

Annie grabbed the top of my left shoulder with her gloved hand and stared at me hard. "Stop it, Gen. You might as well tell yourself an iceberg fell from the sky if you're going to go down that road. Just stop, okay?"

Annie was right. One moment I was grasping on to hope with everything I had. The next, I was attacking it with doubt. "He was right there. We were talking about my car. Then we were at Perry's garage. He said he had to fix a dock at the Pelletier camp. He put his arm around my shoulder and asked Perry to give me a ride."

Annie squeezed my shoulder. "It's okay," she said.

We were still standing outside the command post when we heard the *chuh, chuh, chuh, chuh* of the helicopter. Seconds later, its red light appeared out of the south like an ember. The fog was definitely tearing away, leaving only wispy tendrils in its wake. A handful of people stood around the perimeter of the landing pad, waving large flashlights. I recognized one of them as Warden Gormley. I looked at the clusters of people along the road. I thought of the people inside the command post. I looked at my friend, Annie. My father mattered. Not just to Linda and me and the rest of his family. These people cared about what happened to him. I hoped he would know that. I hoped he would have the chance to see just how many people wanted him to be okay.

CHAPTER
7

The pilot, Randy Haycock, was introduced to us inside the command post. I liked him immediately. He was dressed a lot like my dad—blue jeans, flannel shirt. When we shook hands, his were calloused and strong. He said what he needed to say, then was ready to get on with business.

"So, what else can you tell me?" he asked the lieutenant.

We were standing in a group just in front of the door. Lieutenant Maynard began reeling off the facts—PLS (point last seen), description of the boat, clothing my dad was wearing, GPS coordinates for the Pelletier camp and Sugar Island.

"I'll need two people to fly with me. I want a person on each side of the chopper," Randy said.

"Kathy Gormley, one of our wardens, will go with you, and Anthony Cirillo, one of my deputies," the lieutenant told him. "Hover as low as you can to the camp. Look for anything—the boat, clothing, smoke from a fire. Maybe he's inside the cabin."

"I'm on it," Randy said, his words already trailing behind him as he left.

The lieutenant turned to Linda. She stood with her arms crossed over her chest, her eyes wide and alert.

"I've got three search teams heading out in boats," Lieutenant Maynard said. "The first team will be taking the southern route to the Pelletier camp, which will be island one. The second team will circle around and check out island two, where there's a small camp about a mile due east of the Pelletiers' place. Island three lies about a mile north of the second island. The last team will check it out. Then we'll proceed from there. They'll all be on the same frequency, so you'll hear anything they report back to me."

Linda nodded, small jerks of her head as the lieutenant spoke. She looked small to me, vulnerable.

The lieutenant looked over his shoulder. "Lanette, see if these women want something else to drink. Coffee or soda." He was addressing a woman standing near the radio, whose back was to us. The lieutenant looked at me and then Annie. "You want some hot chocolate?" he asked.

Annie said, "No thanks."

I said, "Sure," having long since finished my coffee. I rubbed my hands together and blew on them, every part of me still feeling chilled.

"You're tired," Linda said. "That's why you're so cold." She lifted her hand toward my face, combed my hair away from my eyes with her fingers. It was the first physical gesture either of us had made toward the other since my father's disappearance. But I didn't want Linda's gestures. Not then, anyway. I felt ashamed of her for God knows what, and perhaps even jealous, as if her grief and concern mattered more than my own.

"Go ahead and have a seat," the lieutenant said. He walked over to the radio. The rest of us gathered around the small table—Annie and I on one side, Linda and Frank on the other. Henry found a spot next to my feet.

"It's seventeen degrees outside," Lanette told us. "No wonder you're cold." She was standing at the kitchen counter, mixing my hot chocolate in a Styrofoam cup. She looked familiar. Stringy dirty blond hair hung below the edges of her thick knit hat, charcoal gray with a white stripe. She was dressed in an oversized men's quilted flannel jacket, blue-and-gray plaid, and black snow pants. As she brought me the cup of hot chocolate, I recognized her left eye.

"You're the new dispatcher," I said.

She handed me the cup. "I just fill in."

Lanette walked back to the radio, where she sat in a folding chair. A computer tech sat beside her.

The lieutenant was now pacing slowly in front of the counter and talking into a handheld receiver. "This is a law enforcement operation. Clear the waterways anywhere near the search. We've got enough people on this already."

I wondered if he was referring to Perry and Annie's dad. And then it hit me. No telling how many other people were out looking for my father. If he were in their shoes, he'd be doing the same thing. To some extent the men where we lived were their own law enforcement, and they didn't want anyone telling them what they could and couldn't do.

There was static on the radio, then Randy's voice. "Command, this is Air One."

"Air One, go ahead," Lanette said.

"I'm over the island now. I'm about fifty feet directly above the cabin. There's no sign of the subject. No boat, no movement inside the camp."

His words numbed me. I looked at Linda. She was staring ahead at nothing, chewing on her bottom lip, scraping it over and over again with her top teeth.

"Air One, this is Lieutenant Maynard at command."

"Command, go ahead."

"What's your visibility?"

"Visibility is at about five miles, with some patches of fog."

"Search over the rest of the island. See if you can see anything."

Some of the islands on the lake were no more than a quarter mile in diameter. Others might be several miles wide. Sugar Island was one of those. It rose up in the open area of the lake on the southeast side, separating Otter Cove and Lily Bay.

The lieutenant called on Air One. "Anything?" he asked.

"I'm flying just above the treetops. It looks like there's a camp on the northwest side of the island."

"Any sign of movement there?"

"Negative. You may want to have your guys do a land search. The island is thick with trees. It's hard to make out much other than the roof."

"Fly over one more time, then go ahead and start a search over the islands due east of the camp. Do a grid search. Work your way clockwise to the shoreline."

Still holding the handset to his mouth, Lieutenant Maynard said, "Boat One, Command."

Again static broke over the frequency. "Boat One, go ahead."

"Where are you now?"

"About a mile just south of the Pelletier camp." I could hear the craft chopping through the water over the frequency.

"Go on to your intended search area and check out the cabin," the Lieutenant said. "If we don't find the subject, we're going to want a ground search over the entire area. Check out the camp on the other side."

The Boat One team leader came back on the radio. "Command, I'll still respond to our initial search area and check out the site."

The lieutenant held the radio handset to his side.

"The wind was blowing steady all night," he told us. "We had twenty-knot gales out of the west. If Mike's not on the island and he was in open water, he could have drifted clear to the other side of the lake, especially if he wasn't anchored all the way down. He may not have been anchored at all."

"He had a hundred feet of anchor line on the boat," I said. "How deep is the water around the island?"

Frank said, "It's pretty rocky around most of the islands. I'm not sure about the Pelletier camp, though."

"We've got a seventy-five-thousand-acre pond out there with a depth reading of over two hundred and fifty feet in some spots. Believe me, that boat could have drifted," Lieutenant Maynard said. The poise he'd seemed to possess earlier was quickly vanishing.

Frank's hands were clasped together on top of the table. He began rubbing his palms against each other, like a nervous habit. "Jerry Stahl is the Boat One team leader," he told us. "He's a volunteer. Lives up at Kokadjo. Knows the lake backward and forward."

"I know the Stahls," Annie said.

"Yeah?" Frank said.

"Yeah. They have a daughter who skis with me."

Annie skied on the high school team. She was good. Her teammates called her the Annihilator. I didn't ski on the school team. I didn't know the Stahls' daughter.

Linda only nodded, acknowledging what was said. Her eyes remained distant.

After a few more minutes, Randy's voice broke the drone of the exchange. "I'm about six miles southeast of the initial search site, about a mile into Galusha Cove. I've spotted a boat that appears to be the one we're looking for." Randy then proceeded to give the coordinates.

There was an intake of breath, maybe mine, maybe Linda's, maybe all of ours. My body went completely still, as if the slightest movement might interfere with what was being said.

"Is there anyone on board?" Lieutenant Maynard asked. He was now facing the table. Linda's and Frank's backs had been toward him. They turned their shoulders so that they could see the lieutenant. He made eye contact with Linda, then me, held the contact with me as we all waited for the pilot's response.

"No, the boat's empty."

The air that I'd been holding tight in my lungs seeped out quickly. A moan literally escaped Linda. Annie laid her hand over my arm, the heat from her palm sinking through the weave of my shirt.

"Give us a description of the boat," the lieutenant said.

Static persisted before Randy's voice was heard. "It's a small, six-passenger craft. Maybe sixteen or eighteen feet. White hull. Windshield. There are two seat cushions. Driver's side and immediate passenger side. Both cushions are bright orange."

"What about any items of clothing? Can you make out anything else?"

"I'm hovering above it at about thirty feet."

Randy paused. Other voices were talking in the background. Then Randy came on again. "There appears to be some kind of box, maybe a toolbox, and some pieces of wood. There's also something yellow on the deck by the driver's side. It looks like a lifejacket or some kind of flotation device."

My dad's boat had orange seat cushions. He kept a yellow lifejacket on the deck by his feet. Linda knew that, too. No doubt, she'd felt the same recognition as I. The skin on her face pulled back into deep wrinkles as her lips pressed into a wide grimace. A high-pitched, eerie moan sounded from somewhere back in her throat. Her body rocked. Frank laid a hand on her shoulder. She startled and immediately pulled her hands from him and into the air as if to push him away. With just as much urgency, she began hitting Frank's shoulder over and over again with her open palms. Frank wrapped both of his arms around her. Linda struggled for only a moment before collapsing into sobs. "Goddamn him," she cried. "Goddamn him."

I knew Linda was damning my father for not being in the boat, for not wearing his lifejacket, for never having worn his lifejacket. She was damning him for not coming home, and damning him even more so because she was afraid he never would.

I understood all of this as I watched her red sweatshirt swell against Frank's large arms. Swell, and then release itself rhythmically. I wanted Linda to stop crying. I wanted to listen to the lieutenant. I wanted him to look at me with his baptismal eyes and give me answers. I wanted to breathe my father's presence back to me, feel him in our midst. And the smell of fear—the acrid, burning smell in my nostrils and inside my mouth—I wanted it gone.

"I can't see anything around the boat," Randy said. "I can fly around, maybe three or four orbits. What do you want me to do?"

"Go ahead and orbit the boat. See if you can spot anything in the water."

The lieutenant held the receiver down to his side and looked away, his jaw sliding forward. Then he brought the receiver back to his mouth. "Command, Boat One, do you read me?"

Again there was static over the radio. "Boat One, go ahead Command."

"Report your location and status," the lieutenant said.

"We're at the initial search site. We've just finished checking out the camp. The cabin is clear. There's no sign that our subject was here," Stahl said. "The place looks like it's been closed up for a while."

"What about the dock?" Lieutenant Maynard asked. "Can you tell if he ever made it to the camp or did any repair?"

"There's no sign of fresh wood or abrasion. Nothing we can see that says he was here."

"Continue with a ground search over the island. Check out the Hamilton camp on the northwest side."

"Ten-four," Jerry Stahl said.

The lieutenant radioed Randy Haycock. "What can you determine about the drift pattern?"

"Looks like the wind was blowing out of the west, but with the islands and the coves, we're not looking at a straight drift pattern. The wind probably took a north direction when it hit the cove. We need to determine the most likely spot where the subject went off course," Randy said.

"We've got point A, the boat launch, and point C, Galusha Cove. We can assume he never made it to point B, the camp," the lieutenant said.

"From the drift pattern, I'd guess he was one to two miles en route before he drifted off course," Randy said.

Why would he have drifted off course? None of this made sense to me. Had the snow blinded him? Had he accidentally gone in the wrong direction? Annie's hand was still on my arm. She gripped it tighter. I looked at Linda, her face dampened and puckered. Frank's arms remained around her shoulders as if trying to hold her together.

The lieutenant sat in one of the folding chairs. He leaned forward with his elbows on his knees. "Continue to orbit the boat. Then check out the shorelines along the cove. Work your way back to the command station," he said.

"Air One, I'll proceed with my search."

I waited for the lieutenant to say "ten-four." He remained quiet. His chin lowered abruptly toward his chest as if emphasizing his frustration. I continued to wait, watching his every move. Except for an occasional sniffle from Linda, Frank, Annie, and my stepmom remained silent.

Again, the lieutenant held the radio to his mouth. "Command, Boat Two."

A handful of seconds passed. "Boat Two, Command."

"Did you get the location of the subject's boat?"

"Galusha Cove. We wrote down the coordinates."

"Head over and mark the exact point of location, then pull the boat back to the command site. Don't try to start it. Just tow it behind you."

"We're about five miles from the point of location. We're heading in that direction now."

More seconds passed. My breathing literally hurt, ached in my chest as I waited.

Then Boat Three called in. "We're at the third island," the leader said. "It's about a mile long. We've conducted a search along the shoreline periphery. We've just begun our ground search. So far we haven't spotted anything, no footprints or any sign that the subject was here."

The man's voice was deep. I thought I recognized it. Maybe I had waited on him at the Lazy Moose.

"Report back to the command headquarters," Lieutenant Maynard said. "We're going to need you to take some men out."

I knew. Maybe it didn't register with Linda or Annie, but I understood what the lieutenant was saying. Perhaps he would have used the word *divers* if we hadn't been in the room. Air One and Boat One and Two and Three weren't going to be looking for my dad anymore. My father, in total darkness, thrashing against a ceiling, away from Linda and me and Perry and his mom. Away from everything warm that he knew. The lieutenant was now changing his plan. He was calling off the search and rescue mission and switching into search and recovery mode. He'd first have to make certain that the boat was my dad's. Perhaps men would continue to operate a conciliatory search along the surrounding shores and island. All those in charge agreed that the boat had drifted. But the mission's efforts would be concentrated on recovering my father's body, not rescuing his life.

CHAPTER
8

Annie and I were standing along the shoreline, waiting for the search team to bring in the boat that had been determined to belong to my father. Linda had stayed inside the command station with Frank.

I'd asked her if she wanted to go outside, but she'd just shook her head and begun massaging the skin around her eyes with her fingertips, as if she'd already cried too much. "I can't," she'd said.

The sky had turned a washed-out blue, softened even more by the thin strands of fog that stretched out over the water like a spider's web. "It's beautiful," I said to Annie.

"What is?"

"The water, the sky. All blended together." For just a second I had experienced a glimpse of peace, like stepping into another dimension, void of any of the chaos. It wasn't until my grandmother's voice rushed toward me from behind that I fell back into reality.

"Oh, mon Dieu! Si'l vous plait, mon Dieu!"

Annie and I quickly turned around. Mémère was breaking through the groups of people, moving in swift steps toward the shore, looking at nothing but the water in front of her. "Please, my Lord!" she continued to plead.

By the time she reached the water's edge, she stood no more than twenty feet from us. Prayerfully, she knelt, cupped her hands together, and dipped them into the icy froth. *"S'il vous plait, mon Dieu, aidez-moi a trouver mon fils. Aidez-moi a trouver mon fils. Mon fils,"* she cried.

She lifted her hands out of the water. Droplets ran down her arms.

Annie gasped and began to cry. I walked over to my grandmother. I knelt behind her and wrapped my arms around her shoulders, pressed my face against the back of her head.

"It's okay, Mémère." And then the knot in my throat relinquished its grip. I held my grandmother tighter, letting my tears disappear into the short strands of her hair. She laid her cold, damp hands over mine, gripped my fingers.

"Mon fils, mon fils," she kept saying. "My son." However, this time her voice had softened from a cry of desperation to the soft, pure gray of sadness.

Feet moved behind me, the small steps of a child. As I looked up, a freckled hand pressed upon my grandmother's head and patted it gently. "Mémère, what's wrong?" I knew Alex's voice. It was the twins' voices that distinguished them the most from each other. Alex's voice was hushed and angelic, almost apologetic. Scott's voice carried, was hoarse and loud at the same time.

Alex bent over and peered into my face. "What's wrong with Mémère?"

I let go of my grandmother and stood and reached for Alex. I hugged him to me, my arms sinking into the down layers of his coat. "She's worried about Dad," I said. "She's sad."

Alex squeezed my stomach against him. "He's going to be okay. He's going to be okay, Gen. Why's Mémère crying?"

The twins knew our father hadn't come home. They knew these people were looking for him. How much more they understood, I wasn't sure.

Annie was now standing beside us. "Yes, Alex. He's going to be okay," she said.

Annie has beautiful blue eyes, and her tears looked like drops of frost.

Alex let go of his clasp around me. He bent forward, supporting his weight with his hands on his knees. This time he peered at my grandmother, whose gaze remained fastened over the water. "Mémère," Alex said. "Don't be sad. Dad's going to be okay. He won't want you sad."

Mémère looked over her shoulder at Alex, her freckles glistening. "Yes, Alex. We must pray that your dad is okay."

I offered Mémère my hand. She took it and stood beside us.

"How did you know they found Dad's boat?" I asked her.

"Perry heard. He called the house."

A breeze blew in off the water, buffeted our gloveless hands. We each shivered and clasped the other's hand tighter.

"Where's Perry now?" I asked.

"He called on his cell. He should be here shortly. He and Josef were riding the shores just north of the Junction. That's when he heard."

Josef was Annie's dad. I knew he kept a radio with him for his job.

Several minutes dragged by, maybe as many as five.

As with the helicopter earlier, we heard the sound of the boat's engine before it became visible. A few more seconds passed and we saw it breaking water around the north side of Lily Bay, just east of Otter Cove. Shadows of people appeared in my periphery, lining the shore around the boat launch. I didn't look at anyone. Their presence existed as no more than a cloud. My reality was Mémère, and Alex, and Annie, and the approaching craft that was pulling another boat toward us.

A couple of men and a woman, dressed in waders and oilskin jackets, walked down the boat ramp and into the water.

A fairly large craft, carrying four men, was approaching. We were standing on the rocky shoreline to the left of the boat launch. The wake swelled into small waves, crashing just in front of us. We waited as the larger vessel made a left turn aft so that the smaller boat being towed was pointing almost directly toward the ramp. There was no question that it belonged to my dad.

"*Oh, mon Dieu!*" Mémère cried.

The people in the water grabbed hold of the towline and untied it from the stern cleats on the search boat. At the same time, to our right, one of the wardens, in a white pickup, began backing a trailer down the ramp.

"How you holding up?" With all of the noise and the people around me, I hadn't noticed Officer Whalen approach.

"Hey," I said. I didn't know how I was holding up.

Annie laid a hand on my back.

I watched the people in the water steer the boat onto the rollers. The warden who had been driving the pickup got out of the truck. He fastened the trailer strap to the bow and began turning the hand crank on the front of the trailer, pulling and securing my dad's Thompson into place.

I stepped closer to the boat. Officer Whalen followed. The yellow lifejacket was right where my dad had left it, on the deck beneath the helm. I had seen him place it there a hundred times, maybe more. Just before he'd turn the key to start the ignition, he'd lift his seat, reach for the lifejacket, and toss it on the deck near his feet, "just in case," he'd said more than a time or two. He'd always made me wear mine, the other lifejacket beneath the passenger seat.

"Were there any other lifejackets on board?" Officer Whalen asked me.

"Underneath the passenger seat," I said.

Officer Whalen and I walked around the bow of the boat, stepping over the hitch. He reached across the side of the hull and lifted the passenger seat. The lifejacket was still there, just as I knew it would be. Both seat cushions were in place as well, just as Randy, the pilot, had reported. Without a lifejacket, my dad wasn't going to be found on the water's surface. At that sheer moment of recognition, I understood why Linda had remained inside the headquarters. Sometimes it's best not to ask a question whose answer you cannot stomach. My stomach began to sour and burn and spasm, and I felt my face film over with a pasty sweat.

Somebody was running, quick, shortened steps. I wheeled around.

"That's my dad's boat! Where's my dad?"

Scott had charged toward the boat. His little hands were now clasping onto the starboard side. He pulled himself up high enough to look inside. "Where's my dad?"

Then I saw Perry, and behind him a group of men

wearing wet suits and carrying tanks, making their way toward the water. Perry walked toward Scott. The divers entered the water, their legs sloshing through to the large search craft, whose engine was still idling. Perry reached Scott, wrapped his arms around Scott's torso, lifted him up and away from the boat.

"Where's my dad?" Scott yelled again, his arms flailing, his legs kicking hard, and his body twisting against Perry's grasp. "I want to see my dad!"

Annie wrapped her arms around Scott's legs. "It's all right, Scott. It's going to be okay," she kept saying.

The divers climbed a ladder that had been hung off the back of Boat Three, the one with the cabin and the search team members. I turned away and bent over. I was going to be sick. Scott continued to yell, "No, I want to see my dad!" I swallowed hard. Swallowed hard again. I couldn't keep it down, the coffee, the hot chocolate, the fear. Officer Whalen held on to my shoulders. I continued to heave even when nothing else would come up. That's when static broke on Officer Whalen's radio and Randy's voice called for Command.

"I'm at four hundred and twenty-three yards on a bearing of three hundred and sixty degrees, straight due north of the boat. There's a shadow in the water, maybe six feet across," Randy told the lieutenant.

I stood, quickly wiped my mouth with my coat sleeve, and stepped away.

The lieutenant called for Boat One.

"Boat One, go ahead."

"Are you at the location site?"

"We're at the site. We've secured the marker buoys."

"Head over to Air One's location. Check out the object. Give me a depth reading. I'm sending divers out now."

CHAPTER
9

"Stay with me," I said to Officer Whalen. I was aware of a change in my voice, as if my words had become completely detached from me. Annie had helped Perry carry Scott into the command station. Mémère and Alex had gone with them. I didn't want to go back into the headquarters. I didn't want to be surrounded by a ceiling and walls, or Linda and Annie and Frank in a booth, each of us hanging on to every word about my father.

Sunlight streamed over the horizon, creating a blinding reflection off of the lake. "I'm right here," Officer Whalen said. "I'm not going anywhere."

We stood to the side of the launch and watched my father's boat being pulled out of the water. The same boat he had first taught me to spin cast from when I was no more than five or six. We'd gone fishing for salmon just after ice out one year in mid-May. I don't think we brought home any catch that day. If we did, I don't recall. But I remember my father standing behind me, his hands wrapped around my wrists as he guided my arms, over and over again, until I got it right.

Sometimes I'd tag along with him to repair docks. Other times he'd let me take the boat out with my friends.

One afternoon in late August a few months back, Dad and I had cut across the west outlet of Moosehead Lake to Indian Pond. It was the last time I'd been on the boat. We'd brought home a stringer of brook trout. I'd cleaned and filleted the fish on a cutting board he'd set up for me on top of a tall stump behind the house. He had to pack up to leave that night for another week at the logging camp. I was still cleaning the fish when he brought his duffel bag out to the truck. Before he left he walked over to where I was working, and sat in an aluminum folding chair. He opened a beer and the two of us talked while I finished cleaning the fish.

"Gen, I've been thinking," he said. "Been thinking about getting me a place on the water."

"Oh, yeah?" I had just finished making an even fillet cut along a fish's spine. I set down the knife and turned around to look at him.

"Been thinking I'd like to wake up and walk out to my dock, have a cup of coffee," he said.

"Taxes are pretty high on lakefront property," I told him, not even sure if he was serious.

He took a long drink from his beer, slowly lowered the can to his knee, and stared off toward the row of spruce trees that line the back of our yard.

"Maybe I'll buy a place on one of the islands. That'd be nice. Have the island all to myself."

He was still staring out toward the trees.

"You going to let others on your island?" I asked.

He chuckled and looked back at me. Then his face softened for a second and his smile smoothed away. He just sat there looking at me.

"What?" I asked.

"Nothing." He chugged a couple quick gulps of his beer, stood, and tossed his empty can into the bin where I was sliding the fish heads and guts. "Help Linda out while I'm gone," he said after he'd already turned and begun walking away.

Standing on the edge of the lake almost three months later, watching my father's empty boat, I realized I hadn't given the conversation much thought at the time, as if his talk of wanting a place on the water was no different than when he'd talk about buying a new truck. But now I wondered. He'd talked about buying a place for *himself*. What had he meant? Or were his words just an accident? Was it a given that the rest of us were included in this new dream of his? And yet it was his look—sweet and sad and childlike all at the same time—that cut into the flesh of my thoughts even more. Was he trying to tell me something? Had I missed a sign?

The white pickup that was towing my father's boat made a right turn out of the parking lot, the trailer bouncing with each rut in the gravel and snow.

"Where are they taking it?" I asked Officer Whalen.

"There's a hangar at the warden's office. My bet is they'll take it there or else to one of the storage sheds, do an autopsy on it, then release it to the family."

The warden's office was in town, down the street from the police station.

"Kind of like my dad's truck," I said.

Officer Whalen laid his hand over the back of my head. I was still wearing my hat. He rubbed my head a couple of times, then dropped his hand by his side.

"When the divers get out to where they found my dad's boat, we'll hear what's going on, right?" I said.

"Everything the lieutenant hears, we'll hear. My radio's on the same frequency."

I dug into my coat pockets for my gloves. "It's getting cold," I told him. "The sun's out, but it's still cold."

"Do you want me to get you a blanket?" Officer Whalen asked.

"No. I want you to stay here," I said. "I want to hear what's going on."

"How's your stomach?" he asked.

"Better, maybe."

Officer Whalen's radio frequency broke a couple of times. We waited. Finally, a voice became clear. "Boat One, Command."

"Command, go ahead Boat One."

"We're at the site, due north of the boat's marker. We're getting a strong echo at a depth reading of approximately thirty feet. We're in about fifty feet of water."

"Go ahead and send a diver down."

"We're sending a diver down now."

"Ten-four," the lieutenant said.

Though I felt a tremor of grief and fear and anguish, and God knows what else, I remained still. So did Officer Whalen. I fixed my gaze on the water's surface, as my grandmother had done earlier.

An object with any weight to it—a log, a small craft, a body—sinking thirty feet instead of fifty feet to the bottom of the lake wasn't so unusual, even with the severely cold temperatures. On one of our fishing trips, I'd hooked a dead lake trout that was drifting beneath the water's surface at fifteen feet. "Why didn't it float, or sink to the bottom?" I'd asked my dad.

"It got itself trapped between the different water pressures and its own combustion," he'd explained, "kind of like its own purgatory."

I didn't give purgatory much thought when he said it. I'd probably never given it much thought; what kind of God would leave a person in limbo?

I looked at Officer Whalen. "Do you believe in God?"

"I do."

"Do you pray?"

"Not as much as I ought to. But, yes, I pray."

"That's good," I said.

I'd gone to church all my life. I'd listened to the priest

and the people around me pray. To some extent, I'd prayed too, mouthed the words in response. God had always felt distant. I didn't want him to feel distant anymore. I wanted him very close, so close that he could hear everything I had to say. It was then that I prayed that whatever was under the water wouldn't be my dad.

"Boat One, Command."

"Command, Boat One, go ahead."

"We've got about a six-foot log drifting parallel with the surface," the team leader, Stahl, said.

"Do you see any other markers? Any items that may belong to the subject?"

"We're not seeing any items from the subject or the boat." There was a pause and more static. "Where do you want us to proceed with our search?" Stahl asked.

"We're going to go back to our estimated point where the subject most likely went off course. Let's begin a dive search there, moving in a northeastward direction," the lieutenant said.

"Do you have an exact GPS coordinate where you want us to begin?" Stahl asked.

"Move in two miles due north of the boat launch and set a marker. Start your dives there. I'll send two more teams out."

It wasn't my dad. My God, it wasn't him. I turned around, noticing the groups of people scattered across the parking lot. That's when I spotted Father Steve standing near the entrance of the mobile home. He was bundled up in a long black coat, a black cap, and a black scarf. I couldn't see his collar, but I knew it was there.

"Father Steve's here," I told Officer Whalen.

"I'd say half the town has showed up. Maybe he can be of some help."

Despite my prayers, despite my need to feel God's presence, the priest didn't represent comfort to me, or hope, or help. My dad had never been big on the church. He'd told Linda she could do the praying and he'd do the paying. I saw the priest as an omen, his black attire a portent to a person's last rites, which this priest had no permission to give.

Then I spotted Perry and Annie walking toward us. Perry was carrying a blanket beneath his right arm. He nodded to Officer Whalen before directing his attention to me. "Hey, Little Bit," he said as he drew closer.

"Hey," I said.

He wrapped the blanket around my shoulders.

"How's Scott?" I asked.

Annie said, "He's still pretty upset. I don't know how much longer Alex is going to hold it together either."

"Maybe it's not a good thing them being here," Officer Whalen said, his words sounding more like a question.

"That's what I was thinking," Annie said. "I'm going to borrow your grandmother's car and take them back to my house. Gina said she'd bring Andrew by to play with them."

Then Annie leaned over and hugged me, and it felt

awkward. It felt like something she did because she didn't know what else to do and she had to do something before she left. I grabbed on to her tightly, both of us wrapped in the blanket, rocked her from side to side until she almost lost her balance. We both kind of laughed.

"Thanks for watching the twins," I said.

"Gen, I'd do anything for you. You know that."

We were now facing each other. "Maybe I'll come home with good news," I told her.

She crossed her fingers on both hands and held them up in the air, took a couple of steps backward, then turned and jogged toward the headquarters, flecks of snow kicking up behind her boots.

I pulled the blanket in snug around my shoulders. Perry moved a step closer to me, like someone about to utter a great secret. I was sure I could feel his warm breath on my face, could feel the life of him through the fabric and air between us.

After a long hesitation he said, "It wasn't Mike. The shadow they spotted. It wasn't him."

I said, "I know."

"That means he may still be alive." Perry looked out over the water, an expression of yearning on his face, as if at any moment my dad might appear, might be delivered up from whatever had taken him from us.

I held the wool over my face, catching my breath, and experiencing the warm dampness on my skin. "Please, God," I whispered. "Have mercy."

CHAPTER 10

Still standing along the shore, Officer Whalen explained the diving process to us. "An anchor point will be set," he said. "Along that vertical line are knots every six feet, and what the divers call spokes. Off of each knot is a rope that swivels around. The divers will make a three-sixty-degree search at each knot. They'll start at about ten feet from the bottom of the lake. They can usually make dives for about four hours before they experience burnout. Then another team has to take over."

I thought I would cry with frustration. "This could take days," I said.

"It can. Days and longer. They're searching in complete blackness. Everything has to be done by feel. It's like diving in an inkwell."

"I just can't believe Mike's out there," Perry said. "Not Mike. He would've made it. I can't accept this without an explanation. How could he have just disappeared from his boat? He hadn't even dropped anchor."

Nobody had an answer for Perry. Nobody had an answer for any of us.

Yesterday my dad had disappeared, and I had no idea why. How could any of this have happened when everything before that moment had felt so normal? That previous spring, I had read in the paper about Christine Bédard, the girl whose car had fallen through the ice. The article quoted her dad: *"She was just here. One minute she's here, the next she's gone. She had just finished eating a slice of meat loaf at the dining room table. Then I'm watching TV, and the cops come by the house."*

He was just here, I thought. He smelled of diesel oil and fish instead of the woodsy smell of balsam and hemlock that I had always associated with him. He'd wanted to buy a place on the water. Why not a cabin in the woods?

Anxiety crawled through my chest and toward my throat like a suffocating scream. I had to break out of there. I had to do something other than wait.

I looked to Perry. "Could you take me to town?" I asked. "Get me something to eat."

"There's food in the headquarters," Officer Whalen said.

"I just need to get out of here," I told him.

Officer Whalen laid a hand over my shoulder. He had always been affectionate like that. Paternal, protective, even with the slightest of acquaintances. "Stop by the headquarters and get a handset," he said. "That way you'll know what's going on and we can talk to you if we need to."

So Perry and I walked back to the command station. I handed him the blanket, then waited outside while he went in to get a radio.

"All set?" Perry asked as he left the mobile home.

I simply nodded.

We walked up the road to where Perry's Blazer was parked.

"Where do you want to eat?"

"I'm not really hungry," I told him.

We climbed into the vehicle. The engine turned several times before kicking in. Perry shifted to drive and eased onto the snow-packed road.

"I was just feeling trapped, like I had to get out of there," I said.

I opened Perry's glove compartment.

"What are you looking for?" he asked.

"Your binoculars."

He patted his coat, just over the large front pocket. "I've got them with me," he said. "You have somewhere in mind you want to go?"

"There's a logging road about a mile from here. It climbs up Pinnacle Point. Do you know where I'm talking about?"

"Logging roads are all over the place around here."

"It's a place Dad used to take me. I thought maybe the two of you had been there before. There's a fire tower that gives a good view of the lake. You can see all of Otter Cove. All of the east side of the lake for that matter."

"I've never been up there," Perry said.

"The road shouldn't be too bad. The snow's dry. When you get to the end, there's a short trail. The tower's hidden in the trees."

My father had told me that he was a boy when he'd first discovered the tower. He'd said that the Forest Service built the tower back in the 1920s, when there used to be logging camps on the mountain. They'd man the post all summer to keep a lookout for fires. When the logging camps closed up, the Forest Service stopped using the tower, maybe thirty years ago.

I was ten when my father first took me up there. We'd gone scouting for white-tailed deer, getting ready for the opening rifle season. Late in the afternoon, after covering a lot of ground on foot looking for signs—scat and the scent of urine, the rubbings in the trees from the bucks' racks—Dad said he had something to show me. He'd said it might help us spot a small herd. "You're not scared of heights are you?" he'd asked.

I'd said, "No." I'd never admitted being afraid of anything, even when fear had slapped itself hard against my chest and found its way into every nerve in my body. I *wanted* to be tough.

The blue sky was gone now, the trees becoming shrouded with a blanket of grayish white.

"Do you think it's going to snow again?" I asked Perry.

"We're supposed to get a couple more inches tonight."

"It's crazy, you know. I always loved the snow. Couldn't wait for winter to get here. But now it feels like my worst enemy."

Perry didn't say anything. We were getting close to the turnoff. "Up here," I told him. "Just ahead on your right."

Perry slowed the vehicle and turned onto a rough-gullied road that carved its way between spruce and birch. The truck listed from right to left and front to back as we climbed up to our first switchback.

"It doesn't look like anyone's been up this road in a while," Perry said.

"Probably not. We'll be making our way to about three thousand feet," I told him.

Kkksshh. Static on Perry's radio. He brought the Blazer to an idle. Both of our bodies leaned forward, our backs away from the cold vinyl seats as we waited, listened for any new word on the search.

More static. No voices.

"Do you think we're out of range?" I asked.

"Shouldn't be. Randy had frequency on his aircraft the whole way from Dover-Foxcroft."

The road ended just in front of a large uprooted tree, as if the tree's fall had marked the end to whatever clearing and maintenance the road received.

"The trail to the tower picks up in the woods," I said as we climbed out of the vehicle.

"You know where you're going?" Perry asked.

"In my sleep," I said.

We stepped over the large deadfall and began walking into a dense patch of birch interspersed with fir and spruce.

"Do you come up here a lot?" Perry asked.

"Not a lot," I said. "The last time I was up here was in the spring. I was watching some osprey that had built a nest on the tower."

"I didn't know you watched birds."

"I'd come up in March and spotted the nest on the platform halfway up the steps. I made a couple more trips in April to look for signs of hatching. I spotted two young and the mother bird last time I was here."

I felt surprise. Come to think of it, I hadn't told anyone about the birds. I hadn't shown anyone the tower before either.

"Over here," I said, stepping through a tangle of vine and young spruce.

We'd found the narrow path that careened through the woods like a game trail.

"Mike always liked the woods," Perry said. "Logging's not easy, but I can't say he complained about it. I think he would've preferred sitting in his delimber out in the woods than being anywhere else."

I was quick to catch Perry's use of the past tense. It wasn't intentional, I knew. It was just the way he talked.

The snow was thickening the higher we climbed.

Even with my Sorrel boots, the snow collected on the bottom half of my jeans and was crusting over.

"Just up ahead," I said. "Maybe another hundred yards."

Our breathing had become noticeable.

Not too much farther and an opening appeared, a clearing resembling a pond of white. In the middle stood the tower, a steel frame with steps that climbed about forty feet to the watchman's cab.

"How could I have never known this was here?" Perry said.

We took sluggish strides through the snow toward the stairs.

"You afraid of heights?" I asked Perry.

"Are you kidding?"

I went up first, with Perry a few steps behind me. Halfway up I pointed out the empty osprey nest, the snow cover giving it an ornamental look.

"Will they be coming back?" Perry asked.

"They're migratory, but, yeah, they should be coming back."

"They're probably down in South America on some beach," he said.

"Probably. It's kind of cool, though. They mate for life. And their eggs don't hatch at the same time. Sometimes they hatch as much as five days apart."

"Makes them seem more like siblings," Perry said.

There was something soft and sad to Perry's voice when he said that. Perry had never married. Though he'd dated, he'd never even come close to walking down the aisle. I knew that he felt closer to my dad than to anyone.

At the top of the tower, the door to the watchman's cab was open. The cab looked like a wooden box with the top half of each wall completely open beneath the roof's overhang. Inside, a dusty layer of snow had blown across the wood floor, gathering in subtle swirls and rivulets.

I stood in front of the opening that faced the east side of the lake. Perry stood beside me.

"This is incredible," he said.

"You should see it on a clear day," I told him.

The sky had definitely changed, becoming dense and wet. The blue had completely vanished, the sun appearing no more than a glint through the heap of dim white that shadowed over us.

Perry unzipped a large pocket on the front of his jacket and took out his binoculars. He glassed the lake, the islands—his body moving slightly from side to side, back and forth, again and again. Then he handed the binoculars to me, and I, too, slowly canvassed the entire stretch of lake before us.

For a moment I thought I spotted a plume of smoke over one of the islands. I continued to watch it, to see if it moved. It didn't. I eventually determined it to be snow on the treetops.

I lowered the binoculars. "Nothing," I said.

We remained silent and still for the next few minutes, as if paying respect to something.

The surface of the lake appeared dull, almost murky, a good indication of the lake's fall turnover. My father was the one who had taught me how to check the seasons of the lake. In the fall, as the surface waters cooled and began losing oxygen, they mixed with the deeper levels, stirring up the stale water from the bottom of the lake. The fish didn't feed much during that time. Those that survived seemed more concerned with coming up for air. Sometimes during fall turnover we'd see fish bobbing to the surface, taking in gulps of air, being strangled by the very habitat in which they lived. After things settled down, the oxygen supply was regenerated. The fish were able to roam and scatter. People didn't fish in the fall. They'd be fined if they did. Instead, they waited for ice cover, after the fish had settled into their winter structure.

As Perry and I stood there, I thought about the cycles of the lake, and what it took for the fish—the brook trout, the salmon, the togue—to survive. And I wondered what it would take for me to survive, as well.

Perry had remained as silent as me, and I wondered what thoughts had stirred or haunted his mind. Maybe he was thinking of him and my dad when they were young, riding their snowmobiles or helping their dad build his garage, or the two of them fighting over girls or at the dinner table. Maybe he was wondering why my dad had never told him about the tower.

My thoughts were on Perry when we heard the noise again.

Kkksshh. This time, a voice accompanied the static.

"Air One, Command," Randy said.

A few seconds passed. Lanette answered the call. "Command, go ahead Air One."

"I just finished flying over the shorelines and some of the smaller islands. We've spotted some ice floe just west of the Galusha Cove inlet. I checked with the Flight Service. Temperatures are supposed to get down into the single digits again tonight."

It was already early afternoon. By four o'clock the sun would be setting. Its heat would be gone. I'd lived in this country all my life and knew what we were up against.

Perry took my hand, so easily I almost didn't notice it.

"Command, Air One," Lieutenant Maynard's voice said.

"Air One, Command."

"I just got off the phone with the weather control center in Bangor. There's another storm coming in out of Canada. How much ice floe are you seeing?"

"So far, we've spotted four sheets, anywhere from three to four feet in diameter." Others were talking on the helicopter. "Hold on," Randy said. A couple of seconds later he said, "Warden Gormley says there's ice forming along the shores of some of the islands. We've covered a sixteen-mile area from the subject's course to the boat's location, extending several miles both north and south of the estimated drift pattern."

"Do a final aerial search around the boat's PLS, then head on back to headquarters."

The boat's point last seen was in Galusha Cove, but where was my father's point last seen? I knew the search and rescue team had marked his PLS as the point where his pickup was found. But who had last seen him? Had someone passed him along the road after he left the garage? Had someone waved and acknowledged him? Had he gone straight to the boat launch, or had he stopped somewhere in town for another cup of coffee? Was anyone else at the boat launch when he put his boat in the water? Had anyone other than Perry warned him about the weather?

All I knew was the point where I had last seen my dad—standing beside me with his arm over my shoulder, his jacket carrying the faint odor of fish and diesel oil. He'd smiled as he'd stood there, a big smile that showed his teeth. His brown eyes glistened from the cold air. He'd sniffed a couple of times, wiped his nose with his sleeve. I'd thought about handing him one of Perry's rags, but they were all stained with grease. "Give her a ride when you're finished, will ya?" he'd said to Perry. I had already turned around to unfasten my coat when he left.

Why didn't I feel some kind of warning? Was there something I'd missed, some kind of sign? Why didn't I talk to him, tell him to be careful? Why didn't I tell him I loved him one last time?

. . .

My father's boat was found on a Sunday morning almost twenty-four hours after I had last seen him. Less than twelve hours later, the lake had begun to freeze, small pallets at first that eventually spread like a growth. By the next morning, the entire lake was one sheet of ice, at least four to six inches deep. If the search crew had been able to determine an exact location for where my father might have gone down, the divers would have continued to work, carving holes in the ice. But as the lieutenant explained, with only a guess as to where my dad might be, a guess that covered miles, conducting ice dives would have been nothing more than hundreds of pricks in the lake's surface, like an overloaded pin cushion.

"Mike Sommer is presumed to be dead," I heard the lieutenant tell a reporter with Channel Four News out of Bangor. He said those words two days after my father had disappeared, the morning the lake had appeared as if hot wax had been poured across its surface. "We will resume our efforts to recover the body in the spring once the lake has thawed," the lieutenant said.

Upon hearing the lieutenant's words, I didn't think of my dad as dead, even if he *was* below the ice cover.

Instead, what I felt was that he was in some kind of hibernation, and eventually he would wake up and come home.

The lieutenant and the reporter were standing in front of the incident command station. Facing them, about ten feet away, stood the cameraman. My father had made headline news in our sliver of the state. People were sitting in their living rooms or around their kitchen tables watching the report *live*, listening to the tragedy of someone they didn't know, and thinking, "how sad." Seconds later those same people would be listening to the sports broadcast, bemoaning the Patriots' losing record or thinking how sad it was that Drew Bledsoe had suffered an injury.

I sat on a damp log just to the right of the command station. I would no longer be told to carry a radio in case someone needed to get hold of me. No one would need to contact me to find out if my dad owned a red coat, or if he carried a third life jacket on the boat. No one would be asking me about my father's and my last conversation. No one would care if I was the last person to see my father alive. I've heard people talk of letdowns, and I know I've experienced them over the years to some degree. The letdown after the Super Bowl or a snowmobile hill climb, a championship ice car race or Christmas. Multiply that by infinity, and perhaps that might come close to describing how I felt, what I saw and experienced and tasted, like something gone bad. Only two days ago, the

Otter Cove public boat launch had been steaming with energy and hope and action, all of which had quickly deflated into a flat line. Headquarters was closing down. The motor home would soon be driven away. Only four vehicles remained.

"Do you believe Mr. Sommer's body is in the lake?" the reporter asked the lieutenant.

"The subject's boat was found on the lake at Galusha Cove. We have no other evidence to indicate that the subject's body is not in those waters."

"Will you drag the lake?" the reporter asked.

"We will continue with our recovery operation in the spring, most likely using our divers and sonar equipment."

The reporter stared directly at the camera. "Thank you, Lieutenant Maynard, for all of your efforts. Our hearts and prayers certainly go out to the family of Mike Sommer." She paused for about a second, as if offering a moment of silence, then said, "This is Jessica O'Donnell, reporting live from Sebaticuk."

Jessica O'Donnell had shoulder-length hair the color of bronze, red lipstick, and fur boots that looked like they'd been turned inside out. She pushed up her sleeve and looked at her gold watch. "Shit."

"What?" the cameraman asked. He was nice looking, youngish, and neatly groomed, with smooth black hair cropped close to his head.

"I'm supposed to meet a friend in Augusta in an hour. I'll never make it."

I watched the reporter take short, shuffled steps across the slippery parking lot. I watched the cameraman follow her. They loaded their equipment into the back of a white van. They climbed into the front. They slammed their doors. They drove off. Six weeks later I saw the reporter again.

ICE COVER

CHAPTER

11

It was a cold, blustery winter day. I was standing on the lake, about two hundred yards from shore, with maybe two feet of ice beneath me. My third race of the season would begin shortly. With the premature ice cover, the season had started early that year, the first race taking place exactly three weeks after my dad's disappearance. Without my father's body, without evidence of his death, I had refused to consider that his life had ended. Sometimes I imagined that he was still around but had simply become invisible—an act of imagination of such force that I almost believed it to be true, as if I could feel him watching me, approving or disapproving of the things I did, even loving me in a strange kind of way. And because I would feel him watching me, I performed better, I tried harder. I performed the little tasks around the house that in the past, before he'd vanished, I'd left unnoticed—tasks like folding the twins' laundry and putting away their clothes, picking up groceries before Linda realized we needed them, dusting my room, being polite. The last was the hardest. There were times I didn't want to talk to anyone, and there were times I wanted to yell and scream and tell Linda to turn off the vacuum, which she continued to run every morning. But I wouldn't yell, because I would imagine my father watching me, and I would force kind words out of my mouth instead, asking Linda if there was anything I could do to help.

It wasn't just the little things I performed better. It was the bigger things. I performed better at my job, as well. My father's paychecks had stopped coming about a month after he was gone, and there was no insurance money because no body had been found. Linda had taken a job as a janitor at the elementary school, but her income didn't cover all of the expenses. It was then that I begged Dorrie at the restaurant to take me on full-time. "What about school?" she'd asked. "It's just one semester," I'd told her. "I can make it up later." As much as I hated to leave school, I had no choice.

My father's disappearance had redefined life as I'd known it, the life with Annie and my friends, as well as the life I'd known at home. Linda missed my father. We all did. But sometimes I wasn't sure she had it in her to go on. I'd listen to her run a bath each night, as if waiting for my father to lumber up the stairs. She'd pour brandy, and from my bedroom I would hear her cry. Sometimes I cried, too, hoping Dad knew how much I wanted him back; wanted his big body moving through the house, making everything okay; wanted his voice telling me what to do, how to fix things. Like the morning the toilet wouldn't flush and Perry wasn't around and we had to call a plumber. Other times I broke down and told him I couldn't do it all, told him I missed him as pure as spring water. But each time I would pull myself back together.

And so when the racing season began, I performed that well, too. I kept going. It was the only thing to do.

"Are you sure you want to race?" Perry had asked me the day I showed up at his garage to paint my car. My father had been gone for ten days.

"I have to," I said.

"Okay, then."

And so we moved on. I painted the car. Perry gave it its final tune-up. When the season opened, we hauled my car out to the racetrack. Life continued around my dad's absence.

Like I said, this was the third race of the season. I'd placed third in the first race and had been only five seconds away from winning first in the second competition. The parking area was lined with trucks and trailers and reconditioned cars, numbered and painted and modified for the day's races, which included five divisions: front-wheel drive, rear-wheel drive, youth, four-wheel drive, and metal-to-ice, consisting of homemade studded tires. It was now close to eleven in the morning. We'd been at the track since a little before eight, withstanding below-zero temperatures and gusts of wind that sprayed our clothes and faces with flakes of snow as fine as sand. People bounced on their toes, jumped in place. Others huddled around the concession stand sipping hot beverages. Occasionally people would climb into spectator vehicles, or the ones used to tow the racing cars, and run their engines and heaters.

The front-wheel-drive division had already finished up. I had competed as the only female in the rear-wheel division and earned one of the eight spots in the final competition, which was about to begin.

I removed my purple hat—the one with long braids down the sides that my dad had given me—and shoved it into my coat pocket. Then I pulled on my helmet and tightened the strap under my chin. I climbed into my Mustang through the driver's-side window and began securing my harness, preparing to line up.

"Hey, Little Bit. You drew number one."

Perry was walking toward me like a snowman with legs, his fleece hat covered with flakes, as was his puffy down jacket. Drawing number one meant that I would be lining up in the front on the inside lane. Coveys of snowmobilers with their machines stood around the perimeter of the track, a quarter-mile oval surrounded by three-foot-high snowbanks.

"A lot of these folks are here to see you," Perry said. He was standing beside the car while I got ready to line up. "This is the biggest turnout we've had."

I wondered if Perry was right. The spectators certainly weren't out there for the cold and wind, the kind that cracked the skin on your nose and froze finger tips, despite hats and gloves and multiple layers of clothing.

"Local Favorite Does It All for Dad." That was one of the headlines in the sports section of the Bangor paper. Like my father, I had made the news. And yet, I was sure the reporters had it all wrong. Yes, I helped out around the house for my dad. I took care of my half brothers mostly for him. In fact, there were many things I did for him. But the racing was something I did for myself. The very acceleration of the car, the speed, seemed to move my life forward in a way that my own body, my own steps, could not.

"Just drive it like your snowmobile," Perry told me, something my dad would always say.

I started the car and eased forward into the lineup of other racers.

"Good luck, Genesis!" someone yelled. I looked around quickly at the crowd. I wished the twins could have made it, but Linda was still bringing them with her to the church on Saturdays. She continued to clean the parish after my father disappeared, despite the fact that she didn't get paid. I wondered if it was her form of penance or tithing since we had no extra cash to put in the offering plate. The twins were getting older. They wanted to go out to the racetrack with Perry and me.

They wanted to see me race. But Linda wouldn't let them have any part of it. Perhaps that was the closest she and I had gotten into a fight since my dad had left.

"Why can't they come with me?" I'd asked her the morning of my second race.

"They just can't," Linda said.

"That's not a reason," I continued.

"Don't argue with me."

Linda was at the sink, rinsing out her coffee cup. I was standing in the doorway to the living room with the twins behind me, Scott holding on to the tail of my flannel shirt, tugging it slightly, as if uttering little pleas.

"I'm not arguing," I said. "I'm asking you a question."

"They're not going. Just leave it at that."

"That's not what Dad would want," I said. With those words, I knew I'd done it. I'd stepped over the invisible boundary, pushed the conversation into the prohibited wilderness.

Linda turned around fiercely, dropping her cup into the porcelain sink. "Don't."

Don't go there? Don't mention my father? Don't challenge her? And so I walked away, feeling like that one small exchange with my stepmom had trapped me in a place I did not want to stay. She was fragile china I had to tiptoe around—expensive china that I'd feel guilty for breaking. And yet there were the twins to consider.

"She'll come around," Perry told me that morning as we drove to the racetrack.

"When?" I asked.

Perry shrugged. "She's just afraid."

"Afraid of what?"

"Of being alone. Of losing someone else she loves. She doesn't want them to get hurt. They watch you race, they're going to want to race too."

But I didn't consider racing dangerous. I wanted to get the twins involved, and I wasn't sure how long their mom would try and protect them. Racing on the ice was the safest kind of racing there was. With nothing but smooth ice under the tires, no matter how sharply a driver turned the vehicle, it would glide rather than roll over. Typically the greatest impact was spinning into a snowbank, unless someone broadsided a car. But even then, the impact was lessened by the fact that there was so little friction between the lake's surface and the car's tires, meaning the vehicle being struck absorbed the impact by sliding.

Now, as I eased onto the track for the warm-up lap, I recognized the reporter from Bangor—the tips of her bronze hair beneath her fur cap, her white parka. She was standing next to the flagman. It was normal for local newspaper reporters to show up at the races, but I didn't recall a reporter from one of the television stations covering the event before.

I gently accelerated, taking the inside lane among the other racers, all of us driving junkyard or backyard cleanups that had been modified. My Mustang had been stripped of its backseat, rear panel, and interior to reduce the car's weight. The back and side windows had also been removed. A boiler plate was added to the driver's side, and safety bars were installed for protection, as well as a five-point safety harness. Truck chains were added to the front wheels and roll chains to the back wheels. For the final touch, I'd personalized my car, Number 42, the same age my dad was when he'd disappeared, and added my own slogan in yellow letters across the hood: "Yes, I'm a girl, and I can kick your butt!"

After we completed another half lap, the flagman swooshed the yellow cloth through the air, and the race began. I was wedged in a tight pack with a black Camaro in front of me and a silver Toyota Corolla to my right. I brought my speed up to forty miles, then fifty as we broke for the first curve. Coming out of it, I brought my speed up to sixty-five, then seventy. The Corolla began to drop back. I steered to the right of the Camaro, again gaining speed. With the fresh plowing just before the heat, the ice was smooth as a mirror. I had the same feeling I always got when I raced, that I was floating. With such little traction, the glide held a mystical quality, as if my body were moving before my mind could catch up.

A car to my right spun out. In my peripheral vision it looked like the Intrepid that had begun the warm-up lap just behind me. It didn't block the course. The race continued without any stops.

By the fourth lap—there would be twelve in all—the

Camaro and I were leading the pack. I knew the Camaro had better acceleration than me. I would have to rely on my skills. I had to outthink the other driver. As we hit the next straightaway, I pushed as close as I could to the Camaro, but as soon as the curve began, eased off the throttle, leaving the Camaro hanging in the front. The Camaro pushed too hard into the turn. When driving on ice, a heavy foot does little but spin wheels, which is exactly what the Camaro did—spun its wheels, slid to the outer edge of the track, barely nipping a Cadillac Catera and anchoring itself in the snowbank.

The rest of the race was mine, and I knew it, feeling a sense of power clear through me. I drove smart, accelerated gently, and let the car correct itself on the spins before I took control of the wheel. At the end of the twelfth lap, I flashed through the finish line with at least thirteen feet between me and the next vehicle.

I took another lap to finish out my deceleration. It was then that I noticed the cheers, heard the whoops and shouting. As I slowed and one of the race officials approached me with the black-and-checkered flag that I would hang out the driver's-side window during my victory lap, a group of people ran toward my car. Spitting snow and clouds of breath accompanied their assault as they clamored onto the vehicle, arms and legs finding their way through the gaping openings—both windows, the back—until five other bodies were packed inside the Mustang along with mine.

Annie threw her arms around my neck, bumping her head against my helmet. "You did it!"

I couldn't believe Annie was there. Over the past six weeks she and I had seen each other only a handful of times. She'd been busy with the ski team. I'd been busy with work and helping with the house and the twins or hanging out at the garage with Perry. There'd been times I'd think about calling her, and yet I wouldn't because either I'd feel too tired to make the effort at conversation or I'd feel this sense of detachment from others that in its own way was satisfying because it required nothing of me.

Annie's younger brother, Trevor, and three other members from the ski team were with her—kids I used to go to high school with before I had dropped out and begun working full-time.

"I thought you were competing at Big Squaw," I yelled over all of the noise.

"Houlton didn't show. Their bus broke down." Annie's face was beaming. "Gen, you did it! You won!" She reached over me and grabbed the flag. With her torso stretched over my lap, she leaned out the window, screaming loud cheers and waving the checkered insignia.

I took off for my victory lap. Some of the spectators had climbed on top of the banks that outlined the track. That's where my dad would have been. That's where he always was at the end of a race. I wished he was there. I wanted him there so badly, I felt as though something as solid and cold as an ax had wedged itself in my chest and was tearing me up inside. I fought the feeling with everything I had. Annie was there. I had won. That had to be enough.

I pulled off the track from the victory lap. Perry slapped the hood of my car, then raised his fist in the air. I parked next to my trailer and opened the driver's-side door. My friends climbed out. So did I. Perry was standing beside me. That's when the reporter approached.

"Hi, I'm Jessica O'Donnell," she said, extending her hand in a tan suede glove. Her other hand held a microphone. The cameraman whom I had seen with her before was standing slightly to her left. The camera was on his shoulder.

After we shook hands, I removed my helmet, holding it to the side, underneath my arm.

Jessica turned around and faced the camera. "I'm standing next to Genesis Sommer, daughter of Mike Sommer, who went missing six weeks ago on Moosehead Lake. We are on the lake at Wharf Junction, where the West Cove Ice Racing Association is holding its third day of races for the season. Seventeen-year-old Genesis has just finished first in the rear-wheel division, competing against seven other racers, all men. Genesis, how are you feeling after such a great victory?"

Jesssica held the microphone toward my mouth.

"It's exciting to win," I said. It *was* exciting, and it was sad all at the same time.

"Did you ever think you could come in first against so

many men? Considering the four heats in your division, isn't it true that you beat out at least thirty other racers?"

I looked to Perry. "Yeah, I guess that's right. I don't know, I mean I want to win when I race. That's what I think about when I'm driving."

"This is your first season without your dad cheering you on. Was it difficult deciding to race again this year without him here?"

"It's difficult not having him here, but it wasn't a difficult decision. It's just something I had to do."

"How does it feel to be racing on the same lake where his boat was found?"

Her question stunned me. For a second I pictured my father's body floating beneath the ice where I stood, and something painful and huge rose up inside me.

"We don't know where he is," I told her.

She appeared baffled by my words, as if she wasn't sure how to respond. I was confused by my words as well. For the past six weeks I had concentrated on getting on with the day-to-day business of living, tasks that had required every ounce of my energy. When I started to get depressed, to wonder, to think about what had happened to my dad, I did something useful, as if I could hear him saying, "Make yourself useful. Be strong." My father's boat was found. My dad was still missing. There were no answers as to what had happened to him.

"People shouldn't stop asking questions," I said.

The cameraman made a reeling motion with his hand. The camera was still rolling.

"Do you think the search should have continued for your father?" Jessica asked.

"I understand why the search was postponed. But no one knows for sure what happened to him. We should still be asking questions," I said.

"Thank you, Genesis." Jessica pivoted her body away from me and directed her attention to the camera. "This is Jessica O'Donnell, where we have been speaking with Genesis Sommer, winner of the rear-wheel division ice race in Wharf Junction, Maine."

The light on the camera went out. The interview was over. Annie tugged my arm. "Let's go," she said.

We walked about ten feet away. "Are you okay?" Annie asked.

"Sure."

"That was kind of weird."

"Why do you say that?"

"I mean, there at the end. Talking about your dad and all. What kind of questions do you think people should be asking?"

I stopped walking. "How could my dad just fall out of a boat? Did he have a heart attack? Was someone else involved? Did he kill himself? How can everyone just accept this?"

"Gen, it's okay. I shouldn't have said anything."

I started walking again, away from Annie and the track.

"Gen?"

"Forget it," I said.

Annie jogged up to me. "I'm sorry," she said.

I stopped and looked back at her friends. A couple of the guys were helping Perry. He'd driven my Mustang onto the trailer. The guys were securing the chains around the car's axles.

"Sometimes, you know, I feel like I can't breathe," I told her. "Like there's all this pressure inside me, all this confusion. When I race, I feel like I can get away from it. But then it comes back. It's just that I don't know what happened to him. People get on with their lives. It's as if he never even existed."

"What can I do?" Annie asked.

"I don't know."

"You want to ride back to my house with me? Some of the guys are going to come over."

I looked out over the track and the cars lining up for the next heat. "I think I'll hang around here. Watch the rest of the races."

"Want to meet up at Woody's later, play some pool?" Annie asked.

"Yeah, okay." Each Saturday after the races, people gathered at Woody's, a local bar up on Shadow Hill, overlooking the lake. "I'll see you later then," I said.

I turned and left Annie and her friends. I kept walking,

all that whiteness around me like a thick cloud. I began a slow jog around to the outside stretch of the track where a number of snowmobiles were parked. Beyond the track, across the lake's seamless white, was a scattering of ice huts, and with those huts, people who braved hours upon hours of the cold to sit and fish. My mind and heart suddenly felt chafed by the very thought of them— people dropping their hooks beneath the barrier that had supposedly trapped my father's body. An image of their hooks snagging my father's flesh or clothing seized me, haunted me.

CHAPTER
12

The flat winter light darkened like a shadow closing in on the day. The metal-to-ice division had just wrapped up its final heat. At this point I was standing near the concession stand after having warmed myself with hot chocolate more than once and a couple of hot dogs. Perry had taken my Mustang back to his garage where I kept it, unloaded the trailer, and returned to the track for the rest of the races. I was about to find him to catch a ride up the hill to Woody's, when Officer Whalen approached me with his snowmobile.

"That was some racing you did earlier."

"Thanks," I said.

"Your dad would have been proud."

I didn't know what to say, but I was glad for his comment.

"You heading up to Woody's?" he asked.

"Yeah."

"Want a ride?"

I straddled the back of his machine and held on to his

torso as he accelerated into the pack of other straggling spectators, all on Ski-Doo or Arctic Cat sleds. Woody's was lit up with strands of colored lights left over from Christmas, striking a painful nostalgia in the center of my sternum. Christmas had come and gone that year like a bad case of pneumonia leaving the lungs and heart weak. Linda and I had put up a tree. The twins had helped us decorate it. On Christmas morning Linda had filled the twins' stockings. That afternoon we ate a small meal at my grandmother's with Perry and Mémère and Mémère's husband, Harry. We came home. The twins went to bed. Linda poured brandy and took a bath. I listened to her cry through my bedroom wall while I lay on my back, holding a pillow to my chest, trying as I might to squelch an ache as strong as a northeasterly wind. The next morning I went to work. When I came home, the tree lay in a heap by the end of the driveway and the stockings were down.

Almost two weeks had passed since Christmas, yet with the snow and the lights that had been left up around town, sometimes it felt very close.

Officer Whalen shut off the engine and we each removed our helmets. "You getting along all right?" he asked.

Though I'd seen him around, he and I had not spoken since the search and rescue operation.

I almost said yes, or that I was getting along all right, or something else that I might have been expected to say, but instead I said, "I miss him."

Officer Whalen laid his hand over my head. The right side of his mouth twitched upward, his face intent.

As we walked up to the entrance, I reached inside my coat pocket for my hat. It wasn't there. Standing beneath the colored lights, I set my helmet on the ground, removed my gloves, and dug deeper into both pockets. I still came up empty.

"Something wrong?" Officer Whalen asked.

"I can't find my hat," I said. "It must have fallen out of my pocket back at the track."

"Take my machine." He handed me the keys. "Maybe you can spot it with the headlight."

"Thanks," I said. I slipped my helmet back on.

I needed that hat. I needed it with a ferocious intensity. At that moment I felt like I would die if I did not find it. I remembered my father losing his wedding ring after my mom had left. He'd recalled having taken it off to wash his hands at some point. He took apart the sink in the bathroom and the kitchen, thinking maybe it had fallen down the drain. I was only five. My mom didn't live with us anymore. I didn't understand why he needed that ring so desperately. I didn't realize that despite my mom leaving, my dad had still loved her. He never found the ring. I think he took the whole thing as a sign. That losing the ring was some kind of message telling him that he was going to have to let the past go and get on without her. I wasn't prepared for that same kind of omen.

The area around the track had completely emptied out by the time I made it back down the hill. I canvassed the parking area, working in a back-and-forth motion, as if mowing a lawn. I stood as I drove the machine, searching the lit pathway. Nothing. Someone had probably picked it up. Maybe that person would return it to me. I'd considered its bright purple and long braids as a sort of signature of mine around the races. Wouldn't someone recognize it and know it belonged to me?

I had jogged around the track after talking to Annie. Perhaps the hat had fallen out of my pocket then. I backtracked my steps, edging forward slowly on the sled, still standing in a straddled position over the seat. As I ventured out farther onto the lake to the opposite side of the track, the air felt colder, the wind stronger, whooshing in gusts. The sky was now dark except for a smear of moonlight through the clouds, allowing me to make out small funnels of snow whirling in pirouettes like ghosts on a ballroom floor—eerie and beautiful. I brought the snow machine to an idle, then shut off the engine, sank onto the seat, and removed my helmet, captivated by the sight of it all, a stillness inside me. The wind moaned and chortled and whined. The cold sunk into my skin like something cleansing. I felt frightened and peaceful all at the same time, as if these funnels of snow dust were spirits rising from the floor of the lake—spirits dancing and laughing and crying.

I'm not sure how long that moment lasted. At some

point I saw movement other than the stirrings of the wind—something dark and solid. For as long as a minute I allowed myself to think that this object, this person, was my father. I allowed myself that imagining, felt it rise from my belly to my heart to my throat before I cautiously warned myself not to go there. Nevertheless, I didn't start the machine and drive off, nor did I continue to search for my hat. I simply remained, watching the swirling particles of snow, listening to the wind, and observing the person, no doubt one of the fishermen returning to shore, as a number of them walked to and from their huts rather than driving snowmobiles.

He was carrying a pail and had a large pack strapped to his back.

"Catch much?" I yelled out.

He walked a few feet closer before answering, the crisp squeaking of his feet through the dry powder on the lake punctuating the whirling sound of the wind.

"Nothing to bring home," he said.

By now he was standing about three feet from the machine. He was tall, maybe six feet, and young looking. He wore a thick knit cap, a dark parka.

"I'm a fishery biologist," he said. "We're doing a creel survey."

I was familiar with the creel surveys. I'd heard my dad talk about them. Biologists collected samples from stomachs of trout and landlocked salmon to measure the food items in them. It had something to do with the reliance on and availability of the smelt population, small fish that had long been the main source of forage for both the salmon and the trout. If the smelt population was down, the other fish wouldn't thrive as well.

"I'm Gabe," he said.

His voice had a soft edge to it. I knew he couldn't be very old. "I'm Genesis. You work for Fisheries and Wildlife then?"

"As an intern."

I nodded. I'd met some of the interns before. Different ones would show up around town from time to time, sometimes staying for as long as a year.

"How far out's your hut?"

"About a half mile. A hundred yards or so into Hungerman's Cove."

"No flashlight?" I asked.

He inhaled the cold air deeply. I watched the cloud of breath slowly escape his mouth. My eyes had adjusted to the darkness, allowing me to see the outline of his face, his broad cheekbones and strong jaw.

"It's nice, don't you think?" he said. "Out here with just the wind and all this space. Besides, I can see the lights from town. I just walk toward them."

I looked behind me at the glitter of light from businesses along Main Street. I could even make out Woody's on top of the hill.

"I guess you're a local then," he said.

"Yep."

"You usually ride by yourself at night?"

"I was racing today." I inclined my head toward the track. "I lost my hat. Thought I'd try to find it."

He hesitated for a moment, seemed to tilt his head to the side. "Sometimes I can hear the cars when I'm out on the ice, unless the wind's really strong. So they let girls race?"

"Yeah."

"Is it a separate division or something?"

"No."

He pivoted just slightly, hesitating again. "That's impressive."

I didn't think of the racing as impressive. It was just something I did.

"I'm heading over to the office now, but I'll be back out in the morning," he said. "I'll keep an eye out for your hat."

I described what the hat looked like. Told him where I might have lost it. My eyes were glossing from the cold, my nose running. Both of us were sniffing. "I should probably head back," I said. "Maybe it fell out in the car. I'll check there. You want a ride?" I asked.

"Thanks, but I'd just as soon walk."

I was getting ready to start the machine when he said, "So what if I find the hat. Where should I return it?"

"Have you heard of the Lazy Moose?" I asked.

"I've stopped there to eat a couple of times."

I looked at his face more closely, wondering if I'd seen

him before, but it was hard to make out anything in the weak light. "I work there," I said.

"Then I guess I haven't stopped in at the right times."

Was he flirting? It startled me, like getting a nudge in the shoulder when standing on slippery ground, and you have to take a moment to reestablish your footing.

"That'd be great if you find the hat," I told him.

I pulled my helmet down over my head and started the machine. The headlight turned on automatically, allowing me to see Gabe more clearly. I guessed him to be around twenty, especially given the fact that he was an intern. His eyes were brown. His face looked soft, almost boyish.

"Where do you go to school?" I asked, my voice loud enough to be heard over the engine. He'd already started to walk away.

"Machias," he said, turning around briefly.

Machias was part of the University of Maine system, a couple of hours southeast of Sebaticuk.

"Maybe I'll see you around." I accelerated the machine slowly and decided I'd canvass the outside perimeter of the track again, making another search for my hat.

Gabe was a biology student. I thought of that as I drove around the track. Thought of all kinds of talks my dad and I'd had when we were out on the boat, or walking through the woods scouting for whitetail, or climbing the fire tower, staring out over the treetops and the lake beyond.

"You ought to do something with your life, Gen. You're smart enough." He'd said that to me more than a time or two.

Another time we'd been hiking along the back side of Scammon Ridge looking for deer sign, deciding where we'd put our tree stands. I was fifteen at the time. I'd hunted with my father since I was ten years old. Whether you were a man or a woman, hunting around our parts was no different than riding a snow machine or casting a spin reel. It was just something you did. We were sitting with our backs against a couple of birch trees hidden by a thick growth of elderberry and gooseberry. We'd stopped to eat lunch.

"You're good in the woods. You understand things."

"What do you mean, I understand things?" I'd asked.

"Well for one, you can find your way into the woods and back out again. That's a start. Just think how many people turn up missing each fall. Most of those folks are from out of state. But even some of the locals wander off too far, get disoriented, don't make it back before hypothermia sets in. You've got this thing called instinct."

He took out an orange from his pack and began peeling it with his thumb. "So I think you ought to do something," he went on.

"Do what?" I asked.

"You're not like the other girls around here."

"How are the other girls around here?" I asked.

"They get married, they have babies. Sometimes they

have babies and then they get married. They work." He pulled apart the orange and offered me a slice. "It's not like I don't want you to have kids. But you're smart. Maybe you could go to college."

"Other kids are smart," I said. "There's kids around here who go to college."

He shoved pieces of orange in his mouth without saying anything. He had that faraway look in his eyes.

"What?" I asked.

"Sometimes when I'm up in the forest, I think of things I might have done different. I mean, I would have had you. Don't get me wrong. But maybe I could have gone to school. And then I think about you. I want you to go to college. Maybe you could study all about the trees or the moose population or the water. You like to read," he said.

"I like to read Stephen King books," I said.

"Maybe you'd like to read other things, you know."

"Maybe."

"I want you to think about it. Promise me you'll think about it, okay?"

I promised him I would. Now, a little more than two years later, I'd stopped going to school. I was waiting tables and reading more Stephen King books. But my dad hadn't held up his part of the deal. Hadn't he promised he'd be there? After my mom left, didn't he tell me he would never leave me like she had? How was I to think about school when Linda and I were doing all we could just to keep the lights on? We'd even canceled our cell phones and had cut back on groceries.

I accelerated the snowmobile, bringing the machine up to forty miles per hour, then fifty, then sixty. Even with my helmet on I could hear the wind howling like something alive. The momentum of the machine surged through my blood, made me feel alive, too. I felt in control for that brief moment. I felt aware. Aware of the wind and the cold and my own fear and confusion, and aware of the power I held with the sled. I drove back to the snow-plowed road that had been carved from the lake onto the shore, decelerating the machine, then turned left onto the road that climbed up to Woody's. I would play pool with Annie. I would accept my trophy for the race. I would go home to a place where neither of my parents lived anymore.

CHAPTER

13

Annie never showed up at Woody's. I waited for her until almost ten. I could have borrowed someone's phone and tried calling her, but I didn't, and I'm not sure I can explain why. In the past I would have phoned her on her cell. She would have apologized and said she'd met up with some of the other kids and lost track of time. But, like I said, I didn't call her, and I can't say that I was angry with her either. Instead what I felt was that something was slowly spilling between us like liquid on glass, and both of us were treading on the hem of that spill, being pushed further and further away from each other. Yes, we'd briefly connect from time to time, like her showing up at the race and riding my victory lap with me. But in the past she would have known what I needed; she would have understood a part of me that sometimes I didn't even understand myself. She would have known that on the night of my biggest ice-racing victory, only six weeks after my dad had disappeared, I needed her to show up at Woody's. I needed not to feel alone in the midst of that crowd, which is exactly how I felt as I played pool with some of the other racers, and as I drank a soda that a female friend of Perry's bought me, and as I received my trophy. Of course I attributed the change in Annie's and my relationship to my father's disappearance and, consequently, to my dropping out of school. And yet I realized that my dad's disappearance hadn't changed Annie's and my friendship as much as it had changed, was changing, me.

Annie and I used to sleep over at each other's houses. We'd build forts with our sleeping bags and pretend we were camping out. We'd lie on our backs for hours, creating tiny moons on our makeshift tents with the beams of our flashlights. We'd talk and laugh and say nothing at all as naturally as bare feet on summer grass. Now, I couldn't feel what I wanted to feel—that sense of freedom to laugh, to feel safe, to feel comfortable, to say what hurt or didn't hurt, to feel a sense of ease around people. I wasn't at ease. I was performing, and I didn't know how to make Annie or anyone understand.

Perry and his friend, Irene or Darlene or whatever her name was, gave me a ride back to the house.

"Good racing, Little Bit," he said as I climbed out of his Blazer.

I looked at the house. The windows were dark. Linda had turned the back light on for me, which meant she'd already gone to bed. "Yeah," I said. "Thanks for the ride and everything."

"Anytime."

He backed out of the driveway. The woman with him waved.

I let myself into the house, unlocking the back door. Linda locked the house up these days, something we never did in the past. I hung my keys and jacket by the door and removed my boots. A bottle of Johnny Walker Red was on the kitchen counter. A third of it was gone. I picked up the bottle. I thought about pouring myself a shot. I'd had Johnny Walker before. I set the bottle down and went upstairs to bed.

The house was cold. We'd agreed to keep the thermostat set at fifty-five. My body shivered as I removed my snow pants and sweater and skimmed down to my thermals. I climbed into bed and buried myself under the covers, tucking my body into a tight ball.

I wished we had a dog. Linda was allergic to dogs. If she wasn't, we'd have one. Annie had a dog, a black Labrador named Lucy, who took turns sleeping with different members of the family. I could use a dog, I thought. Slowly, I began to warm up beneath the comforter. That's when my bedroom door opened.

I poked my face out from beneath the covers. Scott ran for my bed. "Did you win?" he asked, climbing on top of my legs.

"I won," I said.

"I knew it! You really won?" He was now bouncing on his knees.

"Come on. You're going to make me seasick," I said.

He sat back, his legs tucked underneath him.

"You really won?" He asked again.

"Yeah. I really won."

He threw himself forward, wrapping his arms around my neck. "You are *so* cool," he said.

Just as quickly as he'd hugged me, he pulled away, looking at me straight on. "Gen, why won't Mom let us watch you race?"

"I don't know. Perry says she's afraid you'll want to race. He says she's afraid something will happen to you."

"It's all because of Dad, isn't it? If Dad was here, he'd take us."

"Of course he would."

"Gen?"

Scott hesitated as if he wasn't sure he should keep talking.

"What?" I said.

"At church today . . . Okay, you know how sometimes Mom will talk to herself when she's cleaning. Well, I'm not trying to be mean or anything, but she was talking to herself a lot. She was saying a lot of weird stuff."

"What kind of weird stuff?"

He looked down at the sheets. "Angry things."

"What kind of angry things?"

When he didn't answer, I propped the pillow up behind me and pulled him to me. "What kind of angry things?" I asked again.

"She was cussing a lot. She kept saying 'that night in town. *That* night.'"

I felt the muscles in my jaw tighten. "What night?" I asked.

"I don't know, but that's what she kept saying."

"Did she say anything else?"

"Yeah, she said a lot of stuff. But me and Alex, we were in the other room. Gen, I don't want to go there anymore."

"I'll talk to her," I said.

"She's crying a lot, too," Scott said.

"I know."

"She's not the only one who misses him. Alex and me, we miss him a lot."

"I know you do."

I pressed my face against his hair. It smelled sweet and clean. "You had a bath," I said.

"No. I had a shower."

"Since when did you start taking showers?"

"I don't know. A couple of days ago. *You* take showers."

"Yeah, I do. Sometimes I take a bath."

"Yeah, but most of the time you take showers."

I laughed a little. "You better get to bed."

"Promise you'll talk to her." Scott was now sitting forward.

"I promise," I said.

. . .

I had to be at work at six the next morning for the breakfast crowd. I woke early, a little before five, showered, and dressed in a pair of jeans and a green-and-navy flannel shirt. Linda and the twins were still asleep when I left. The bottle of Johnny Walker was no longer on the counter.

I kept my father's truck plugged into the garage at night to keep the engine from freezing. I unplugged it before climbing in, primed it a couple of times, and turned the starter. I'd been driving the green truck for almost five weeks, ever since Warden Gormley had returned it to our house along with my dad's boat. An autopsy had been done on both, which had required each member of the family to be inked and printed. Inland Fisheries and Wildlife said the truck and the boat had come out clean, meaning no fingerprints other than those of family members had been found. There were no signs suggesting foul play in my father's disappearance.

The boat was now parked on its trailer behind the garage at our house and covered with a large blue tarp, and though the boat was out of sight, I felt it there, larger than it actually was, like a phantom casting a shadow over everything I did, whether reading a book or working a puzzle with the twins or falling asleep. Only when I left the house did I escape its looming spirit. I never discussed this with Linda, and I could never have brought myself to suggest we sell the boat, or that Perry or I, or someone, should haul it away. As much as I hated the darkness of its presence, it was still a piece of my dad's life that I couldn't let go of.

With his truck, things were different. It didn't haunt me but rather comforted me. When I drove it, I felt in control and connected to my dad in some kind of spiritual way. It reminded me of the conversations he and I would have when we'd traveled the snowmobile circuit when I was younger. Or all of the Saturdays over the past few years when we'd hauled my Mustang onto the lake for ice races. It reminded me of my father driving up into the northern ranges for work. And sometimes I would cry, as if my tears were rain slapping onto the windshield, making it difficult for me to see, and even that would make me feel close to him. It wasn't my father's truck that had taken him away.

I drove to Perry's garage before going in to work. After my dad's disappearance, Perry had given me a key. My Mustang was parked inside. I searched it thoroughly for my hat, my nerves still feeling disheveled from having lost it. It wasn't there, which meant it had to have fallen out on the ice. If I didn't have to be at work, I would have headed back out onto the lake. I'd search again when I finished my shift.

The Lazy Moose was several blocks from the garage—just around the corner and down Main Street. I parked behind the restaurant and entered through the back door. Tony, Dorrie's boyfriend, was cracking eggs over the griddle on the far wall.

"Hey, Gen, congratulations," he said.

"Thanks, Tony."

I set my boots underneath my coat and slipped on my sneakers. I loved the smell of the restaurant in the mornings—bacon and sausage and coffee, the smell of grease on the griddle, the faint smoke. Linda Ronstadt was playing over the stereo.

"Gen, they got you on the news last night." Dorrie walked into the kitchen from the dining room. She clipped up an order. "Over easy, but she doesn't want them runny."

"What the hell does that mean?" Tony said.

"It means soft, Tony." I'd just finished tying my shoes.

"We were watching the ten o'clock news," Dorrie said. "Just about to turn the thing off and get some sleep, and then that woman came on. Isn't that right, Tony?"

"She's telling the truth. We were sitting right there."

Dorrie had owned and operated the restaurant for the past fifteen years. She'd bought it with the money her husband had left her after he'd died. I guessed she had to be somewhere in her sixties, though she'd never tell her age.

"That's something," she said, shaking her head. "I told Maura this morning, we got a celebrity."

Maura was one of the other waitresses. She worked weekends.

"I bet your mom sure is proud," Dorrie went on. "How's your mom getting along anyway?"

People had referred to Linda as my mom for years. It had always bothered me. It bothered me more now. "She's fine."

Dorrie lined ketchup bottles on a tray to bring out to the dining room.

"Big crowd yesterday?" I asked her.

"*Psshh*, you're telling me. People coming in all day long from the race. Had a couple of touring clubs off the trails. One group was all the way up from Rhode Island."

I picked up my pen and order pad. Winter had come early. Most of the locals would be in good shape, especially the business owners. The more snow the better as far as they were concerned. They couldn't survive on summer tourism alone. I wondered how long the cold and snow would drag on into the spring.

I followed Dorrie out into the dining room, which seated about twenty to twenty-five people. It was at least half-full. Maura was already on the floor taking orders.

Most of the customers were snowmobilers getting a warm meal before a long day on the trails. Some of them were locals whom I recognized. A handful of the diners were from out of town, probably downstate around the Portland area, or even as far as Massachusetts or Connecticut. They were easy to pick out—cleanly shaven men, women with makeup, all of them wearing brand-name snow gear. I liked waiting on the tourists. They left larger tips.

People continued to trickle in. Others left. I'd worked at least a couple of hours, making small talk with the customers and Dorrie and Maura, when the intern showed up, taking a seat at one of the tables by the bar.

"I'll take this one," I told Maura.

Maura was plump, with long, frizzy brown hair pulled straight back into a ponytail. She looked at Gabe, then me, raising her eyebrows inquisitively. Maura liked gossip, and I knew I'd be next on her list.

I walked up to Gabe from behind and placed a menu in front of him. "Coffee?" I asked.

"Hey," he said, turning in his seat. "I've got something for you."

I could see him better in the restaurant than out on the lake in the dark. I liked his looks. He had strong features despite something boyish in his eyes. He wasn't wearing a hat, though it was obvious he'd worn one earlier that morning. His light brown hair was thick and matted and somewhat on end from static electricity. He had full lips, a nice smile. He was handsome in a plain sort of way.

He was wearing a green parka. He dug down into one of the pockets and pulled out my hat.

"No way!"

The hat was damp, no doubt from melted snow and ice. I sat in the chair next to him. "Where did you find it?"

"It was along the bank of the track. Pretty much right where you were looking, but the snow was covering most of it. You would have never found it in the dark."

"I was going to head out there later today after my shift. Thanks," I said.

"No problem."

I started to get up, but then I felt my eyes pulled back to him. He was watching me. The next moment we were both grinning, acknowledging some kind of silly awareness of each other.

"Where are you from?" I asked.

He rubbed his hand over his head, as if trying, unsuccessfully, to straighten out his hair. "Portsmouth."

"New Hampshire?"

"Yeah."

"That's a long way." Anything outside of Maine seemed like a long way to me.

"Five hours. Not bad."

A couple more customers walked in. "I should get back to work," I said. I stood up and scooted the chair in. "Do you want anything?"

He ordered a cup of coffee and the southwestern omelet.

I picked up my hat from the table. "Hey, thanks again."

Back in the kitchen, Dorrie gave me the eye. Either she'd seen me with Gabe, or Maura had said something to her.

"What?" I said as I put my hat with my coat, all the while trying to conceal the makings of a smile.

"I didn't say anything."

"You didn't have to." I passed Gabe's order on to Tony, then went to check on the other customers.

Maura was standing by the coffee machine, refilling her carafe. "He's watching you," she said.

I picked up the second carafe. I didn't have to ask Maura who she was referring to. I'd felt it too, noticed it from the corner of my eye. I was curious, but also skeptical. I didn't usually draw that kind of attention. In other words, I wasn't the kind of girl guys watched unless I was on the racetrack. My dad used to tell me I was pretty. He said I was natural, low maintenance, the kind of woman a guy would like to wake up to one day. The guys I knew weren't interested in *low maintenance*, which, for the most part, had suited me just fine.

I poured Gabe a cup of coffee. "So, are you staying around here?" I asked.

"Another intern and I are renting an apartment next to the Boom Chain."

"You grab breakfast there a lot?"

"Sometimes."

The Boom Chain was one of the only other restaurants in our area. I used to go there with my dad. We'd grab breakfast before we'd take his boat out to Mt. Kineo. He'd get talking about the logging industry back when his dad had moved down from New Brunswick.

Back when the logs were dragged down the rivers and lakes to the different mills rather than being hauled by trucks. The logs were corralled by a chain fastened to boom sticks, then pulled by a boat. The chain mechanism was called a boom chain. It fascinated my father. Sometimes he thought logs should still be moved that way. He didn't like all the trucks barreling down the highways. At times my dad seemed old-fashioned, or just simple in a pleasant sort of way.

I went to check on Gabe's order. When I brought it out to him, Annie was standing by the bar. I set down Gabe's order and joined her.

"Sorry I didn't make it back to Woody's," she said.

I looked over my shoulder to see if Gabe could hear anything. People were talking, the music was playing. I decided he was too far away.

"It would have been nice, you know."

"No, really. I'm sorry, Gen. But something came up."

"It's okay."

"A bunch of us went back to my house. Then one of the guys talked us into going sledding up at Conifer Ridge. There were some other kids up there from Rockville."

"It's okay," I said again, though I was looking away as I said it.

"Hey, Gen, we got to talk," she said. "When do you get off?"

She seemed in a hurry, like she wasn't comfortable being there. "About what?" I said. "What's up?"

Annie looked around at the customers. "Not here."

"I've got a break coming up in about twenty minutes," I told her. "I can meet you around back."

Annie nodded her head slowly. "Yeah, okay."

"You all right?" I asked.

"I'm fine. I'll see you around back."

I took the orders of a couple more families that had come in, all the while wondering what was on Annie's mind. I checked on Gabe, offering him more coffee. He'd taken off his coat and was wearing a long-sleeved green thermal, the sleeves pushed up a ways. I liked his build. Muscular but not bulky. He looked strong.

"No, I'm good," he said. "I've actually got to get back out on the lake."

"Do you always work weekends?" I asked.

"Every other. I switch with the other intern I'm living with."

I wrote him his ticket. "See you around then?" I asked, raising my eyebrows just a little so he'd know it was a question.

His chin rocked forward as if he was going to say something else, then he smiled funny—sweet, bashful, embarrassed. I wasn't sure.

"What?" I asked.

"Thought maybe I'd watch you race sometime," he said.

"Yeah?"

"Yeah. If that would be okay."

"Yeah, sure," I said. "It can be a long wait, though. Between the divisions and heats."

He pushed his plate forward and crossed his arms on the table. His hands looked calloused, like my dad's, and his cuticles nicked. "I'm used to waiting," he said. "On the ice, that is. Sometimes that's all we do is wait."

"Okay, so I'll see you around?" I said.

We looked at each other for a couple more seconds.

"Yeah, definitely," he said.

I picked up his dishes and carried them back to the kitchen. When I returned to the dining room, he was gone, having left his money on the table with the check.

I looked at my watch, headed back to the kitchen, and removed my apron. My coat and hat were hanging by the back door. I layered and walked outside to the alley. Annie had showed this time.

"So, what's up?" I asked.

She took a deep breath. A funnel of steam escaped her mouth.

"Come on, Annie," I said.

"Last night some of the kids were talking. One of them brought up your dad. It was this red-haired kid from Rockville. I didn't know him. He said the whole search thing was just a waste of time. That your dad had pulled the whole thing off."

"What are you talking about?"

"That's what he said. He told us there was this guy in

{ 139 }

Rockville who had worked with your dad at the logging camp."

"What did he mean, my dad had pulled the whole thing off?"

"The kid was drunk and talking big, so I don't know. Trevor had been telling everyone about how you had won the race. Then this kid wants to know if you're the one whose father went missing. That's how it came up."

"What else did he say?"

Annie shoved her hands in her coat pockets and ground the heel of her boot into a frozen pocket of snow. "That was pretty much it. I just thought you should know."

Annie wasn't telling me everything. I don't know how I knew it, but I did. The inside of my mouth suddenly felt numb. "Come on, Annie."

"No, really. That's all he said." She shoved her heel harder into the snow. "I shouldn't have even come here. It's probably nothing, okay?"

Annie started to walk away.

"If it was nothing, you wouldn't have come by here," I said.

The soles of Annie's boots squeaked against the packed snow as she turned around. "I'm really sorry, Gen. For everything, you know."

"Yeah, me too," I said. "What was his name, the kid who was saying that stuff?"

"Eric or Aaron. Something like that. I don't remember."

"And he's from Rockville?"

"Yeah. It's not true, though. I mean, he was just talking. But it was your dad. I just thought I should tell you what people were saying."

"Yeah, you should have told me. You can call, you know. When you hear something, or come by the house."

"We drove by your house," Annie said. "But the lights were out. I guess it feels kind of weird with Linda and all. I mean, I hear she's not doing so well. And with you not having a cell."

I took in a deep breath, felt the cold sting my lungs. I looked down the alley, watched a couple of cars creep along the street at the alley's end, listened to snowmobiles start up from around the front of the restaurant. The snowpack was enough for snowmobilers to drive down the streets. They'd park along Main Street for something to eat or drink, then start up and head right out onto the frozen lake, where a lot of them would eventually detour off into the woods.

"I better go," Annie said.

I didn't know what to say. Linda *wasn't* doing well. No one in the family really was.

"Hey, thanks for coming by," I said.

Annie took a couple of steps toward me. She wrapped her right arm around my shoulders. Her hug felt tentative. Kind of like the one at the search site, neither one of us really knowing what to say or do. Nothing felt natural anymore, not even brushing my teeth or pulling on my boots or talking to my best friend.

I watched Annie walk away, listened to her boots grind into the frozen layer of snow covering the alley until she'd rounded the corner and was out of sight.

The sky was a dingy white. From a distance church bells rang. I didn't go to church anymore. Instead I went to work. I still prayed, though. I prayed for my dad, prayed that God was taking care of him. I thought about what Annie had come to tell me. Thought about the red-haired kid and what he'd said. Thought about all the times I'd prayed as if my father was alive. Now people were talking as if he was. I wondered what else this kid had said. It would be easy to find out who he was. All I had to do was ask around. That's what Annie wanted me to do. That's why she'd told me he had red hair. There was a reason why she hadn't told me everything. Like it was something she didn't want to get too close to. People were like that around where I lived. If they got too uncomfortable, they'd just keep quiet. Instead, Annie had given me enough information so I could find out for myself.

I picked up a piece of clean ice from the ground, pressed it between my lips, letting my skin stick to the dry, cold surface until the ice melted against my tongue. Maybe Dorrie or Maura would know who he was. If not them, then one of my customers would.

CHAPTER
14

Eric Pellerin worked with his dad up in Rockville as a carpet layer. He'd graduated from high school the year before. I'd found out who he was from one of my customers just before my shift was up.

I'd waited on several people that day from Rockville. I'd asked each of them if they knew a red-haired kid up that way, about my age, by the name of Eric or Aaron.

"That'd be the Pellerin boy," Shirley Monson told me. Shirley had come in with a couple of her grandkids. "He's working for his father now."

As soon as my shift was up, I checked the phone book in the back. There were two Pellerins listed in Rockville. I called the first one. When I asked to speak with Eric, a man said, "That's my grandson. You've got the wrong number." He then proceeded to give me Eric's telephone number, which was the same for the second Pellerin listed on Kearsarge Road. When I called it, the phone rang for a long time, but no answering machine or voice mail picked up. I jotted down the address.

"You looking up that customer who was in here?" Dorrie asked.

"And what customer would that be?" I asked. I was already putting on my coat and hat.

"You might could use someone to get your mind off things," Dorrie went on. She was putting together a plate of fish and chips. "Sometimes a man can be a healthy distraction."

I was swapping out my sneakers for my boots.

"I'm just saying, with your dad and all, might be nice for you to have someone to take your mind off things," Dorrie told me.

I pulled my hat down over my ears. It had mostly dried out by now.

"Thanks for the advice." I finished fastening my coat. "I'll see you guys tomorrow."

"Hey, Genesis, seriously. You need anything, you let me know, okay?"

Dorrie was giving me the kind of look I imagined a mother giving a daughter. The kind of look Annie's mom gave her. The kind of look my own mother might have given me if she'd stuck around. Linda didn't give me those kinds of looks. We'd never had a mother-daughter sort of relationship. I think my dad had hoped we'd at least be friends. I didn't see that ever happening. The only thing Linda and I had in common was my father, and now the twins. Of course my own mother and I probably didn't have a lot in common either.

My mom walked out when I was six. I have no other memory of her before that day, no remembrance of a time she and my father were together, no remembrance as to the kind of mother she was to me. But I do remember sitting on the left arm of the sofa, staring out the living-room window, the sky a thick lead gray. My hair was long, even then, like my mom's, and I was chewing on the ends. Sometimes I think I can even remember the metallic taste of my hair in my mouth, can feel the gritty texture of the ends between my teeth. My mom was wearing blue jeans and a rust-colored suede coat. I can conjure the way that coat smelled, like cedar and hide and her perfume. I think she was wearing boots with thick heels, because I remember the sound of them against the icy sidewalk that led to her yellow car. I don't recollect her getting into the car or seeing her drive away, or Perry sleeping on the sofa that night, or Mémère fixing dinner. Those were details I overheard years later.

I learned that after my mom walked out, she moved to Worcester, Massachusetts, where she had grown up. Now she lives in Portland, about three hours south of here, where she works at the airport for one of the car rental companies.

Her name is Mary. Other than the details I could recall from the day she left, I didn't know anything about her firsthand. My picture of her was only from what I'd hear Mémère say, and word of her was dropped in my presence about as often as tropical rain in December. Mémère got her information from a woman who was friends with my mom. They'd worked together at a bar at one of the lodges on the west side of town. I guess this woman and my mom still kept in touch from time to time. If Mémère was in the mood, she'd pass the information on to me. I suppose Mémère thought I should know these things. "After all she *is* your mom," Mémère would say. But I really didn't care to know. I'd rather believe I came from someone else who didn't choose to leave but instead who died heroically from cancer or who had been struck accidentally by an oncoming vehicle.

I hadn't always felt this way. There was a time I wanted to know more about my mom; I wanted to believe that she had loved me and that she was good. I'd imagine her pushing me in a swing or licking cake batter with me from the beaters of a mixer. I imagined her like every other mom I knew.

I was about the same age as the twins when I first learned how my mom and dad met. He'd started dating Linda. I was intensely jealous of Linda at first. I'd created a picture of my mother in my mind in hopes that it would push Linda out of my life. One morning my father and I were sitting at the kitchen table eating cereal.

"Do you ever miss her?" I'd asked him.

"Who?"

I felt angry that he had no idea who I was talking about. "My *mom*. Do you ever miss my *mom*?"

He left his spoon in his bowl, leaned back in his chair. "No," he said. "Not anymore."

His voice was calm, so I decided to ask him more. "What was she like?"

"It's been so long, Gen. Honestly, sometimes I'm not sure I can remember what she was like."

Even now I couldn't say that I believed him. Instead I understood how a person tried to control memories, ignoring certain ones like ignoring an unpleasant piece of food on a plate or an unpleasant person at the grocery store. "At least tell me how you met. What did you like about her?"

My dad had his hands on his legs, his elbows pressed outward. "Well, she wasn't from here. I can tell you that. I think that was part of the problem."

"Where was she from?"

"She was from Massachusetts, a place called Worcester. She'd taken a summer job over at the lodge on Kineo."

Kineo was mostly a summer resort, other than a handful of private cottages. The Oak Lodge had been around for as far back as I could remember.

"So, she was just there for the summer?"

"Yep."

"And you guys got married right after that."

"Not right after. We lived together for a while. Thought we'd get to know each other better, and it was cheaper that way, with her not having a place of her own."

"So, what did you like about her?" I asked.

"She was a hard worker," he said. "She liked to laugh. She was fun. I don't know. We were young. It was a long time ago."

My dad never said much else about my mom. A couple of years later when I was in Bangor shopping with Mémère, I sprayed the different bottles of perfume from a counter in one of the stores, trying to identify my mom's scent. After about six bottles, I found it. I applied some to my wrists, thinking maybe the scent would help me to remember something I'd forgotten. By the next morning when the scent had worn off, I still couldn't remember anything about my mom except for the day she left. Perhaps it was then that I accepted something that I have never gone back on. Leaving was her choice. My father had chosen to stay.

. . .

My shift was over at two. I didn't drive back to the house. Instead I turned left onto Highway 15 and 6, driving north toward Rockville, a small town situated on the northwest tip of the lake. The roads weren't too bad. They'd been heavily plowed. I knew the Rockville area fairly well. There was a boat ramp just off the center of town that gave access to one of the shortest stretches on the lake to Kineo Island. My father and I had launched the boat there numerous times. And once in the winter, when the lake was frozen almost two feet deep, we'd hiked across that stretch. The General Store in the center of Rockville offered hot lunches. Sometimes Dad would bring Linda and the twins and me up there to eat. Kearsarge Road wasn't far past the store. I'd seen the sign.

The Pellerins' house couldn't be difficult to find. Maybe Eric wouldn't be home. No one had answered the phone. But I at least had to try.

The drive was still, and quiet, and fresh. Even when I approached the town, its vacant roads and vacant vehicles parked in front of lifeless houses and buildings left a similar stillness to that of the woods I'd just driven through. I passed the General Store. A dim light shone from inside. Shortly past it, I turned onto Kearsarge Road. After about a hundred feet, I came upon the big yellow house, initially hidden by tall spruce trees. The driveway and yard were littered with old vehicles. A couple of chickens were running loose in front of a side porch that sagged from the main structure of the house. About a quarter mile farther down the road was a brown colonial with patches of grayish white where the paint had peeled, resembling snow. The windows were covered in film-coated plastic. Two snowmobiles and the skeleton of a third were parked out front, but I didn't see any other vehicles or lights on inside the house.

Nevertheless, I pulled into the driveway, approached the front door, and knocked. A dog barked from inside, but after a couple of minutes, it settled down. I walked around the house, stepping beside rusty automobile parts and five-gallon pails turned upside down and frozen in the snow, resembling perfectly shaped cobblestones. I might as well have been stepping on familiar ground. Though my dad had prided himself on keeping our house and yard "intact," which meant a place for everything, including whatever scraps he may have accumulated and saved for a grander purpose someday, junkyard parts and chickens and snowmobiles and dogs were the typical lawn ornaments in our parts. By no means was any of this a sign of laziness, but rather it was a sign of people who worked with their hands and left pieces of their labor wherever they lived. It was only because of the white-collared tourists who bought up large parcels of our land and built lofty homes with triangular windows and yards too perfect to be lived on that I knew the difference.

As I knocked on the back door, the dog resumed his barking. Still, no one answered. I decided that with the dog in the house, someone would be home before too long.

I climbed into the truck, backed out of the driveway, and drove the half mile or so to the main stretch of town. A couple of people were leaving the General Store. I pulled into an open parking space and rolled down the window, and as I did, one of the men nodded his head in my direction, seeming to understand that I wanted to ask something. He was middle-aged, with a dark beard, and was carrying a cup of coffee. The man behind him was younger and had a hood pulled up around his head.

"Do either of you guys know Eric Pellerin?"

"You looking for him?"

"Yeah, do you know where I can find him?"

"Just seen him over at the docks, hauling in a string of trout. He and a friend of his."

"Hey, thanks."

"No problem."

I drove about a mile toward the public boat ramp, where I knew the local docks were. For the most part, the edge of the shore around the town had a steep and rocky pitch. A lot of the fishermen approached the ice from the boat ramp or one of the docks. A green Ford Ranger passed me. Its muffler was either busted or missing. The driver was youngish, with red hair. Another guy was in the passenger seat. I turned into the next driveway I came to, backed out, and turned around. The Ranger had parked in front of the General Store. I parked beside it and went in.

I spotted the two men at the front counter, where they were purchasing drinks.

"Is one of you Eric?" I asked.

The one with red hair turned around.

"That'd be me."

"Hey." I held out my hand, thick glove and all. "I'm Genesis," I said.

He shook my hand, turning his chin a little to the side as if saying, "What is this all about?"

"Could I talk to you?" I asked.

"Yeah, sure. Hold on."

Eric turned around to finish paying for his drink.

"Come on," he said, now holding a Powerade in his left hand and walking over to one of the booths.

Eric and his friend sat on one side of the booth. I sat across from them.

"What's up?" Eric said.

He wasn't what I'd pictured or expected. I'd pictured one of the typical guys I knew who sawed off mufflers and opened up throttles. Maybe he was one of these, but something about him gave the impression that he was more than that as well. He was tall and lean, with thick, wavy hair. His face was neatly shaven, with sideburns about an inch below each ear. His body, his gestures, seemed serious and deliberate.

"You were with a friend of mine last night," I said. "Annie Therriault."

"You said your name was Genesis?"

"Yep."

"You're the one who wins all those car races?"

"I win some races," I said.

"That's really cool."

"Thanks."

"Hey, this is a friend of mine, Tom Garvey."

Tom extended his hand over the table. "How you doing?"

"So you needed to talk to me?" Eric said.

"Annie said you knew something about my dad."

Eric still had not opened his drink. He had his hands clasped together in front of him and was looking at me dead-on. He didn't answer right away.

Then he dropped his chin and shook his head. "Geez, I'm sorry. Now I remember."

Slowly he looked up, his face still serious. "It was a wasted night. We don't usually get that bad. A bunch of us had gone out. But, yeah, I remember your friend."

"Do you remember what you said to her?"

"Yeah. I'm sorry. I mean, I shouldn't have said anything. It's not my place, you know."

He looked at his friend. "Tom, you were there. Remember how we were talking about that guy on the lake?"

Tom opened his drink. He wasn't as good looking as Eric. He was small boned, appeared lanky despite his layers of clothing, with a gaunt face and stringy black hair. "Yeah, man. Tough break. That your dad?"

My throat suddenly felt like a collapsed door.

"Seriously, Genesis, you got to be hurting. I'm really sorry." Eric still hadn't touched his drink. His eyes were a dark green, as dark as the needles of a spruce, his eyelashes a rich brown. I'd never seen such beautiful eyes. They almost haunted me.

"Do you know something about him? About what happened?" I asked.

He leaned back, slouching a little in his seat. "People talk, you know. Something like that shit with your dad happens, you hear things. I got my tongue all liquored up last night, started running my mouth."

"Annie says your dad knows some guy who worked with my dad," I prompted.

His expression didn't change. He still didn't say anything.

I was frustrated. How was I to get this guy to talk? I planted my elbows on the table, buried my forehead in my hands, digging my fingers beneath the wool of my hat. I stayed like that for a couple of seconds. No one was saying anything. Then I pulled my hat from my head and looked up. "Come on, Eric. If you know something, you got to tell me."

"You really want to know?" Eric said, now looking at me again. Those eyes of his could paralyze my blood—with what? Fear? Control? Because he knew something I didn't?

"That's why I'm here," I said.

Eric leaned forward over the table again. He held his drink in both his hands. "I'm not saying it's true. But, yeah. My dad knows this guy who says he worked with your old man. Says this woman started working at the camp. I don't know, maybe out of Quebec or one of those towns around there. This guy says your dad had something going on with her. Made it sound like your old man was looking for a way out."

I knew what he was saying, but I didn't buy it. "What else?" I said.

"That's it. Something like that with your dad, people

get all revved up like they don't have anything better to talk about or do with their lives."

"Like you last night?" I said.

He looked away only briefly, then shot his eyes back at me. "Yeah, like me last night. So this guy's thinking your dad and this woman had something planned. Says a guy doesn't just disappear from his boat."

"This friend of your dad's, you know him?" I asked.

"I know him some. How well does anyone know another person?"

With those words, I felt like I had just sipped something toxic, felt it burning its way to my stomach. My dad was different. He kept his life organized. His clutter might as well have been catalogued, as well as his thoughts. And those thoughts, the kind that were so hard to get to sometimes, were shared only when he was ready, as if his mind were some kind of calculated dispenser. I'd learned to like him that way. Liked that in his own way he'd set himself apart from everyone else.

"Does he have a name?" I asked. "This friend of your dad's."

"Marc Suter."

"And he works at the camp?"

"Used to," Eric said. "He's trading shifts somewhere down in Millinocket now. Passes through here every once in a while."

"So in other words, chances of me tracking him down are pretty slim," I said.

Eric opened his drink, took a couple of slow swallows. "Yeah, that's about right," he said. "Picks up different jobs. Doesn't have anything steady. The guy's getting up in age. Doesn't have any family. But he's okay."

My hat was wadded up in my hands. "Meaning you believe him," I said.

Eric shook his head. "No, I'm not saying that. Like I told you, people talk. But he wouldn't have made up the part about the woman. I mean, he was up there, you know."

"Would your dad have any idea where I could find this guy?"

"I'll ask him. See if he knows anything else."

"Yeah?"

"Yeah. Sure. This whole thing's gotta suck for you."

I pulled my hat back down on my head. "Thanks," I said. I thought about what Eric had told me, about the possibility of another woman in my dad's life. And then I said, "My dad's wife . . . she's not my mom. My mom left a long time ago."

What was I trying to say? Was I trying to give my father an excuse? Was I trying to tell Eric that what he'd said was okay, that if it was true, it didn't hurt me as bad as he might have thought, because, after all, it was only Linda my dad would've been going behind? Was I betraying my own father by even saying such a thing? My dad had a family. He had me and Scott and Alex. And he had Linda. He drank brandy with her and they laughed and talked and he kissed her long and held her when he'd see her after a shift. He never would have left us. Maybe I didn't know all of him. But I knew him well enough.

"I gotta go," I said. I started to slide out of the booth.

"You got a number?" Eric said

I was sitting on the outer edge of my seat. I looked back.

"You wanted me to talk to my dad. You got a number so I can call you?"

"Yeah, sure," I said. "Sorry."

"Hey, Tom, you got a pen on you?" Eric asked.

Tom reached inside his coat pocket and took out a pen. Eric pulled out a napkin from the dispenser on the table. He slid the pen and napkin in front of me.

I hesitated. "You won't say anything to anyone, will you? To my stepmom or anyone?"

"I'm not saying anything to no one. Like I said, I'm really sorry about last night."

I wrote down my number, yet when I gave the napkin back, I felt something close to guilt. Giving Eric a way to reach me meant I'd bought in, if even somewhat, to what he'd told me, as if I'd forgotten about my dad watching, and suddenly I felt like I had let him down.

· · ·

Driving back to Sebaticuk, I noticed the light angling over the lake and trees like the dull glow of a flashlight about to go out. Strange, perhaps, but I felt as though all of my imaginings and conjuring of my father's presence, my refusal to believe that he was dead, had somehow preserved him, had kept him alive. I also recognized that to feel this hope meant a part of me had believed Eric, and a part of me chastised myself for that. It meant I was willing to believe that my dad had betrayed Linda. Had betrayed all of us. Would it not be better if he were dead? No, I decided. If my father were somewhere, breathing and moving and existing, I would find him, and he would explain it to me, and everything would be all right. He would have a story with as much weight to it as the heavy, wet snow around me. The kind that can be shoveled and moved and pushed away. The kind that the sun eventually melts as late spring arrives. So, I looked at the light, tried to hold on to it, even after it diminished over the western slope of land bordering the lake.

CHAPTER
15

Back at the house, Mémère's car was parked in the drive-way. She stopped in a couple of times a week to check on things, "to prop Linda up," she'd tell me. Maybe Mémère wasn't so different from me—behaving in a way she thought would please my dad. He would have wanted Mémère to check in on Linda, to hold the family up, so that's what she did.

Secretly, I wished Linda was stronger. But I also began to understand that perhaps it was her weakness that had drawn my father to her. His first wife had left him. Linda would never do that. Maybe that's why he hadn't minded her not working out of the home. Linda needed him, as if he had been carrying her on his shoulders, and now that he was gone, she was having to use her legs for the first time. What I felt for Linda was pity, not love. And pity was a painful, uncomfortable feeling to bear.

Linda and Mémère were sitting at the kitchen table when I entered the house. They were drinking coffee and going over bills. I'd seen this sight numerous times since my father's disappearance.

Mémère set down her cup when she saw me, got up and greeted me, kissing me on both cheeks, then squeezing me strongly against her. "How was your day? Good? Good," she said, never waiting for me to answer. A smile beamed across her face, tightly carved into her freckled cheeks. Her green eyes glistened. Even her skin glowed. Her very presence brought life to the whole house, as if someone had just turned on the light. There it was again—the thought of light. I wanted what Mémère had. I wanted her passion and vigor. I touched on it when I was racing, but something about me always felt washed out, sad. Racing was my way of trying to change that. It made me feel alive.

"I'm fixing spaghetti tonight. I make good spaghetti, you know. My spaghetti is *so* good."

Mémère had us over for dinner several nights a week. She insisted. She'd bring food by the house, too. I knew Mémère and Harry didn't have much money either, but she would never let on to that now. Families took care of each other.

Mémère patted my cheeks with her warm palms, then hugged me again before she turned back to Linda. "So we're all set?" she said, looking back at my stepmom, who was staring down at the pieces of paper in front of her. "You know what to do?"

Linda nodded vaguely.

Mémère would help Linda organize the bills, help her identify which ones to pay first, which ones to pay in full, and which ones she could make payments on. And I knew Mémère helped her pay them also—slipped some in her pocket to take care of on her own.

"So I'll see you in a couple of hours?" Mémère said, looking at Linda.

Again Linda nodded.

"Good." Mémère put on her coat, her scarf and hat and boots, and as I watched her I felt the weight of even ordinary things, of getting dressed, of eating, of paying bills, of getting on. The very tangibility of our actions.

Linda was still sitting at the table, staring at the bills, when Mémère left. I hung my coat by the door, removed my boots, set my sneakers beside them, the ones I wore at work. I joined Linda at the table, wanting to read her face, wanting to see if I could understand anything more about what Eric had told me.

"Hi," Linda said, not looking at me.

"Hi," I said back.

And then she did something she'd never done before. She reached over and held my hand.

"How was work?" she asked.

"The same."

I tried to think of something to say to her. The TV was on in the den. Some kids' show. I thought of the twins, no doubt spacing out in front of the television, perhaps dozing off like they would sometimes do. I wanted to say they shouldn't be watching so much TV. They should be out sledding or riding snowmobiles or racing cars. They should be playing Lost in the Wilderness like Annie and I used to do. And then there was the thought of Annie. I would have to call her later. We were slipping apart. I knew she'd felt it too.

As I sat with Linda, felt her hand over mine, the subject of another woman in my dad's life seemed very distant. Even if it were true, Linda would never believe it. I realized that the love she felt for my dad was pure, almost innocent. It was the real thing. I could never let her know about Eric's and my conversation.

Scott and Alex began laughing at something on TV. I thought about Scott's and my conversation the night before. I'd promised him I'd talk to Linda. Maybe now was a good time. I at least had to try.

"Can I talk to you about something?" I asked her.

Linda let go of my hand, wrapped her fingers around the empty coffee cup in front of her. "Sure."

"It's about the twins," I said.

Did I imagine it, or did her body recoil, pull even deeper into itself?

"We need to talk about this," I told her. I had a feeling she knew what was coming.

"They want to come to the races," I said. "Why won't you let them go?"

"We've already talked about this," she said.

"Not really," I said. "We haven't really talked about it. Why won't you let them go?" I asked again.

Linda didn't say anything. She just kept staring at her coffee cup.

"You can't keep doing this to them," I said.

It was then that Linda's eyes shot up at me. "Doing what?"

My jaw clenched. I took a deep breath. And then I said it. "You're turning them into sissies. You're not going to protect them by always having them with you," I said, remembering what Perry had told me. "It's not going to work that way. You'll turn them against you."

"They're just children," Linda said.

"They're *boys*. They'll be eight soon. I was racing snowmobiles when I was their age."

"I don't want them racing."

"We're not talking about them racing. But you can't hide them from the world. Why can't they go with Perry and me? Do you know how many kids are out there?"

I leaned back against the spindles of the chair. And then it hit me. "You wouldn't know, would you? Because you've never gone."

"That's not my fault," she said. "That was always your and Mike's thing."

For just a second, maybe not even that long, I felt something in Linda's voice. Had she resented me, too? Had she been jealous of me, as I, for so long, had been jealous of her, a jealousy I hated to even admit because it felt so trivial?

"It *is* Dad's and my thing," I said. "But you could have come too. You could have watched even if it was just one race."

I wasn't sure I was getting anywhere.

"Let them go," I said.

"I can't."

"Why?"

And then she cried. I hated it when she cried.

"If you keep treating them this way, you'll lose them," I said. "They won't want to be around you."

"I'm so afraid," she said. "Of everything. That if I let them go, they'll get along without me."

I sat in that moment, in that kitchen, at the oak table with bills and coffee cups and fingerprints, with the smell of damp coats and a faint lingering of the previous night's dinner. And I heard something for the first time, something that left me feeling guilty because I had not recognized it before. Linda wasn't so afraid of the twins getting hurt. She was afraid of not being needed, of fading like the light I had witnessed earlier.

"I was nineteen when I met your dad," Linda said. "I'd never even been on my own. It was exciting. I thought anything could happen."

I knew how Linda and my father had met. He'd been running a ferry on the weekends in the summer when the logging was slow, carrying people from Wharf Junction over to Kineo. Linda and her family had rented a cabin off of Lily Bay Road. They'd take the ferry over to the island. Not long after they left Sebaticuk, my dad was driving back and forth to New Hampshire. I'd stay at Mémère's. Eventually Linda moved in with us, "to make things easier," Dad had said. I was only seven. By the time I was eight, they'd decided to get married. Linda wanted to have kids. It was the right thing to do, Dad had told me. So, Kineo had played a part in both of my dad's marriages.

I looked at Linda. She appeared older to me than she had six months before. I thought back to a time when I'd been sitting on the rear patio, a small patch of stonework that my father had once laid. Thought about watching her hoe the twenty-by-forty-foot garden in the backyard—large enough to produce vegetables for dinner, but just small enough for her to manage. Her long, strawberry blond hair had been pulled back into a ponytail. She'd been wearing shorts, and I remember thinking she looked too young to be married to my dad. But now, sitting across from her in a house that we kept too cold these days, she looked older, tired, and at that moment, I wanted my dad back, if for nothing else, than for her.

Linda was wearing a thick cardigan. She pulled it in closer around herself. I felt the cold too.

"I'll check on the stove," I said.

Though the basement was still warm—the earthen

walls definitely provided insulation—when I opened the stove, the fire had indeed burned down to smoldering ash. I rolled up newspaper, added extra kindling. The embers slowly ignited the paper, and eventually the thin pieces of wood. I waited for the flame to grow, watched its changing colors, from a warm orange to red and finally to an iridescent blue. Then I added the logs. The whole process was peaceful and warming and so natural, I could almost sink into its reverie as if falling into another world, one of comfort and completion.

I watched the flame for a while before closing the stove and returning upstairs, listened to it hiss and pop, listened to the wood snap. The phone rang. I could hear Linda scooting out her chair, could hear her footsteps as she walked over to the wall mount by the refrigerator to pick up the receiver, her voice, and then footsteps as she walked toward the basement door.

"Gen!"

"Be right up," I said.

Linda was standing at the top of the stairs with her hand over the phone's mouthpiece. "It's a boy," she whispered as I approached her.

I immediately assumed it was Eric and was shocked that he'd gotten back to me so soon. I took the phone and walked through the den where the twins were lying on the sofa in front of the TV, their faces like zombies'. They might as well have been sleeping with their eyes open. I then went upstairs to my room.

"Hello?"

"Genesis?"

"Yeah?"

"It's Gabe."

His voice startled me. "Hi," I said, and then, "How'd you get my number?" I wasn't even aware that he knew my last name.

"I stopped by the restaurant after I got in off the ice. I asked the woman you work with. Is that all right?"

"Yeah, that's fine." I hesitated for just a second, still registering that he'd called me. Then I added, "People around here aren't too hard to find anyway." It was okay that he'd called. It was okay that he'd asked for my number. I didn't want him to think otherwise. "What's up?" I said.

"I thought maybe we could get together. Maybe I could take you out to eat?"

"Yeah, okay," I said. My thoughts felt foggy, congested, and yet, this guy wanted to take me to dinner, and that was nice.

"Tomorrow night?"

"Okay, sure."

"Should I pick you up, or do you want to meet somewhere?"

I was now sitting on my bed. I looked to my bedroom door as if seeing Linda, even though she was still downstairs. "Let's meet," I said.

"How about Kelly's Landing?"

"Sure."

"Around seven? I don't usually finish up at work till after six sometime."

"Yeah, seven's good," I said. "I'll see you then."

I turned off the phone and sat in my cold room on my cold bed for maybe a minute or two. Just sat there, like when hitting pause while watching a movie.

I looked at the phone. I snapped out of it. I'd told myself I'd call Annie. I tried her number. "She's not here, Gen. Still at ski practice," her mom said. I'd forgotten. Annie had school and ski team practice and homework. Annie had a life that was completely different from mine.

I went downstairs, stepped onto the sofa between the twins, and dug my legs underneath the blanket that was covering them. Both of them stirred. Scott sat up and leaned into me. Alex slid his toes underneath my knees. The three of us stared at the TV, watched the Disney Channel, waited for Linda to say it was time to leave, to head over to Mémère's. Maybe Linda would join us on the sofa. Maybe we could all just sit together and watch TV.

CHAPTER
16

It was sometime on the way back from Mémère's that it hit me. We'd sat around the table at her house, we'd eaten dinner, we'd talked about the winter we were having, we'd told Mémère how good the spaghetti was. We never mentioned my father. It was as if history had already been written and we had to accept the chronicles, despite the fact that huge gaps lay in those chronicles. "Mike Sommer is *presumed* dead," the papers had said.

Of course I thought of what Eric had told me on the drive to Mémère's, during dinner, on the drive home. I wanted him to be right because I wanted my father to be alive. I also wanted to prove Eric wrong. Suddenly, I knew what I had to do.

I had never been to the logging camp where my dad had worked. None of us had. It was simply my father's place of work. He'd get in and out of there as quickly as he could. The only people my dad ever talked about from up there were other men, some of the Canucks, as he referred to them—the Canadian workers—and the cook, whom my dad said he got along with real well.

So when we got back to the house, I dug around in the back of my dad's truck for his map, tucked it into my pocket, then went inside the house and upstairs to my room. I knew St. John's Camp was off the Golden Road, the main thoroughfare for pulpwood cut on more than half of the couple of million acres of Maine forest owned by Great Northern Paper. The road, mostly gravel and rock, runs west from Millinocket to Saint-Zacharie, Quebec, at the Canadian border. With it being winter, the Golden Road would be tricky enough. Getting to it would be even trickier. I would have to drive twenty minutes northeast to Kokadjo, a town only by name, as a mere seven people lived there, according to the last census, then wind my way through four-wheel-drive trails. I took out a piece of paper and jotted down the rest of the directions. *Left at Kokadjo on logging road. Stay on road until it splits. Go left onto Greenville Road. At the T in the road, take left onto Golden Road. Long way. Follow signs for St. John's Camp.*

There was no hesitation in me whatsoever. The trip was as necessary as food or sleep. Why had I not gone up there before, especially since my dad went missing? The smallest bit of information would be worth the effort. Even seeing the place where my father had spent so much of his time would be worth it. If I left early, I could easily make the two-hour drive there and back and still be home in time to meet Gabe.

The only problem was that I was scheduled to work the next morning. I picked up the phone in the hall, walked back to my room, and called Dorrie. "You told me to let you know if I needed anything," I said to her. "Something's come up. I know it's short notice, but I really need tomorrow off." I didn't want to lie to her, to pretend I was sick.

"I'm sure we can cover for you. Mondays are usually slow. What's the matter?"

"Nothing's the matter. Please, Dorrie."

"You don't want to talk about it. That's okay. We'll see you Tuesday then?"

"Thanks, Dorrie."

. . .

I awoke the next morning with something like a fragile pulse thrumming against my palms, thrumming inside my chest, making strange music in my head. Anticipation and fear of finding something, and of finding nothing.

I turned off the alarm before it went off. It was barely five o'clock. I would be driving during the moose's prime feeding time. They, too, would be stirring from slumber, making their way out of the timber in which they'd bedded down for the night, and grazing salt along the roads. I'd have to drive cautiously.

Not wanting to make too much noise, I decided I'd shower when I returned. I also packed only a bottle of water, deciding I'd pick up some food in Kokadjo at the general store.

The thermostat just outside the back door read a perfect zero. The snow reflected starlight like the silver scales of a fish. It would be a clear day, and I was thankful for the weather.

Mounds of snow embanked the dark road as I drove out of town. At times I felt like I was maneuvering my way through a ditch. More than once eyes stared back at me from the rim of the snow, and halfway to Kokadjo a moose came close to stepping onto the icy pavement immediately in front of me, but at the last second, hesitated just long enough for me to pass. Moose typically didn't stop for vehicles. Signs along all of the highways in northern Maine warned motorists of moose crossings, as well as "High Rate of Moose Crashes." Locals knew to heed the warnings.

I pulled up to the small general store and restaurant in Kokadjo close to six thirty, just as the sun was climbing over the horizon. Already a group of snowmobiles and a few trucks were parked outside the brown clapboard building. A small trucking rig was parked off to the side.

I had ten dollars with me—enough to buy breakfast and a sandwich for later. I pulled out a chair at a table in the corner. Before I'd had a chance to look around, a waitress approached me. I ordered the daily special— eggs, bacon, toast, and coffee. It was only then, after I'd handed the menu to the woman and she'd turned to walk away, that I noticed the other diners. The snowmobilers were easy to pick out—a rowdy group of men in black nylon bibs and turtlenecks. A couple of wardens from Inland Fisheries and Wildlife were sitting across from each other, elbows on the table as they drank their coffee, both appearing seriously engaged in their conversation. I thought of Gabe. I was glad I would be seeing him later.

Only one other person was eating alone. He was no doubt a logger, wearing nothing more than a thermal top layered with a flannel shirt, and a pair of Carhartt pants. I knew from my dad that the loggers didn't bother with coats. Coats were considered too cumbersome, and the work itself provided enough heat to warm the body. I wondered where this man was headed to. Wondered if he knew my dad. There were a number of jobber camps and company camps in the area. Jobber camps were owned by contractors. Company camps were owned by Great Northern, the same organization that owned the majority of the land. St. John's Camp, where my dad worked, was a company camp.

The man was eating pancakes, shoving forkfuls into his mouth. He looked up from his plate, his jaw working the food, and stared straight back at me with a kind of thoughtful look, like he was trying to figure something out.

He had bushy eyebrows, black and gray, and bushy hair the same color. Most of the loggers headed over to camps on a Sunday night, beginning their week at four in the morning on a Monday. I thought about this man's schedule. Maybe he wasn't a logger.

After the waitress brought my food, I ate in a hurry. I left money on the table before my check came and stood to go. I didn't stop at the store just adjacent to the dining room. I didn't purchase a sandwich. It wasn't intentional. I was simply nervous, eager to get to the camp, and I forgot.

No more than one hundred feet past the store was the turnoff I needed to take to get to the Golden Road. As I made the left, I quickly recognized that I would need to switch the truck to four-wheel-drive low. As soon as I had the truck on a straight path, I put it in neutral, then engaged the lower gear. The turnoff route, wide enough for only one vehicle, was snow-packed, which allowed for some traction. I would have to steer a straight path or I would be stuck.

After a couple of miles, the road, if it could even be called that—perhaps a better word for it would be *trail*—approached a steep hill. I climbed it steadily, the back wheels of the truck spinning out a couple of times and the bed beginning to fishtail. The hill covered at least a quarter of a mile. At the top the land opened up, offering a beautiful panoramic view of the forest, as well as Big Spencer and Little Spencer mountains. The sky was now a smooth blue, the groundcover as white as cotton, unsullied by traffic or sand or salt. And before me, just over the crest of the hill, was a steep decline that seemed to barrel out at the bottom into a frozen gully where the trail then began to climb once again. Even if I approached the decline in neutral, I would have to carefully brake and steady the steering wheel to keep the truck on the narrow path. I would also need to make sure I gauged my acceleration accurately, giving it just enough gas as I came out of the gully so as to catch traction on the other side and make it up the next hill. I had not seen another soul since leaving Kokadjo, not even a deer or moose. This was not a place I would want to get stuck.

I began my descent. The day was still early. The sun had not yet softened the surface of packed snow. I steered straight down the middle of the hill, touching the breaks only briefly, not wanting to lose control. At the bottom, the wheels glided easily over the frozen gully. As soon as my front tires hit the next bank, I began to press the gas pedal gently until I felt the pull of traction. The next hill was a much easier climb, and the route seemed to eventually level out, winding its way through the trees. But then there was another obstacle. The path I was on suddenly forked, with each of my two choices at least two feet narrower than the trail I was on.

I put the truck in park and checked the map. It didn't show a fork in the road. I then climbed out of the truck to look at my choices more closely. The trail to my right showed no tire tracks. The trail to the left showed thick tire-tread markings like those made by a large logging truck. I found it hard to believe that trucks of that size could fit on these back-forest roads. We had not had snow for a couple of days, so perhaps the tire marks were two days old. They were frozen to the touch, so I knew they weren't fresh. I decided to take the path with the tread marks, gauging the other path as nothing more than a snowmobile trail.

I thought I had been making good time and estimated that I was about an hour and fifteen minutes from the Golden Road. It was a beautiful day. I would enjoy the scenery. I would try not to think about anything other than the land around me. I drove on. I spotted a few deer, a fox, a couple of rabbits. A hawk flew overhead. More than an hour had passed. I still wasn't at the Golden Road, nor did I see any indication in the land that I might be approaching it. I had no doubt taken the wrong fork in the road. I looked at my watch. Almost nine o'clock, the same time I'd hoped to pull into camp. I had no choice but to backtrack—another hour back, then an hour and a half or more toward the camp. And of course there was the problem of turning the truck around. I thought I remembered a small patch of clearing about a half mile behind. I switched into reverse, rolled down the window, and leaned my head out. I would have to back up. I listened for oncoming trucks but heard nothing except my own engine.

Sure enough, the clearing was where I had remembered it. Though the snow at this spot was softer than that on the road, I was able to maneuver the turnaround without getting stuck. I was definitely anxious about my wrong turn and eager to get to the camp. I wondered what I would say when I got there, how I would be received. I decided that my first approach would be to say that I had come to pick up my father's things. After that point I would be able to ask some questions. But who would I talk to? The men would be in the woods until dark or a little after. I knew from my dad that the men put in twelve-hour days, packing their lunches at three or four in the morning before they headed out.

Someone would be around, I decided. If nothing else, I would talk to the cook, a man by the name of Owen, who my dad said managed the place. Owen was the only person who had been there as long as my father had—twenty-two years. Typically the workers hung on only a few years before moving on to something else. Maybe my dad stayed on because of his love for the woods and the solitude. Or maybe it was because he had a daughter to support and eventually a wife and two sons. Or did I dare acknowledge maybe there was someone there he couldn't be without?

I thought about all of these things, all of the long years my dad had worked in the woods, the numerous drives he'd made to the camp. I tried to do the math in my head, just how many miles he'd covered, but got lost somewhere in my counting. Finally I was back at the fork. I made a lot of start-and-stop turns until I had the truck steered toward the trail on the right. It now showed fresh trail marks. All I'd have to do is keep my tires in the tracks.

The rest of the drive was less eventful. At last I came to the T in the road and spotted the sign for the Golden Road. I felt as if I had just landed in civilization. I waited for two large logging trucks to pass before I made my left-hand turn. It was public knowledge that the logging trucks on any of these roads always had the right of way. One of the rigs that passed was half the length of a football field, pulling three trailers loaded with tree-length logs. The sun was now beating down, turning the road's surface into a layer of slush over ice. And my dad's truck could use new tires.

About a mile into the course of the road, another large rig came up behind me, barreling down much faster than the speed limit of forty-five miles per hour. Instead of slowing toward me, it whipped around me, the vacuum of its momentum forcing my truck toward the shoulder. I began to lose control in the thick slush, certain I'd get stuck. My tires weren't picking up any traction. I switched to reverse, gave the truck a sharp acceleration, stopped, then shifted back to drive, again giving a quick surge on the gas, rocking the vehicle back and forth until it dislodged and eventually spun over the shoulder slush and was back on the road. At this rate, I didn't think I'd ever get to the camp. And I was hungry, wanting the sandwich I'd intended to buy at the store. Maybe there would be something to eat at the camp.

As I continued down the Golden Road, I thought of all the accidents that could have befallen my dad: the commute in blizzards and below-freezing temperatures, the logging trucks that claimed the road despite who might be driving along, the moose whose eyes did not catch the glow of headlights and reflect it back. Out of all the things that could have taken my father from me, out of all the risks he'd exposed himself to, why would it be the lake that would prove his greatest challenge?

At last I saw a sign for St. John's Camp. More logging rigs passed me, though traveling at slower speeds. The woods around me were more chopped up, gouged and cleared, with slash and limbs piled haphazardly. Just ahead was the entrance sign for the camp. At the top of a hill, I approached a large opening in the trees. I had made it. I checked my watch. It was already noon.

On one side of the opening was machinery, from skidders to logging trucks to plows and graders. There were propane tanks and metal sheds where, no doubt, more equipment was stored. There was also a fueling center and a generator shed. To the right of the opening were three white trailers with blue trim. Everything looked deserted, yet pristine and organized. I pulled up in front of the middle building, turned off the truck, and got out. A small wooden sign beside the door said "Dining Hall" in white letters. I would go inside and look around, see if I could find anyone, though I had this awful nervous feeling that I was trespassing, that at any moment, someone might walk out of the woods with a shotgun. The silence was almost unbearable. I experienced a shivering certainty that I could hear the snow that lay on the ground, hear it breathing, feel it watching me.

I opened the dining hall door. "Hello," I called out.

I thought I heard a noise from somewhere in the back of the building. I called out again. "Anyone here?"

On each side of me were long benches, and beneath the benches were all kinds of slippers. I almost laughed, picturing men as large as my dad traipsing around in moccasins and fleece booties.

Hurried tapping sounded against the wood floor. Within a minute a medium-sized black dog was trotting toward me, its tail wagging ferociously.

"Hey," I said, kneeling down to greet it.

I was looking at the dog, my face taking its share of licks and welcoming.

"Boozer likes company," a man's voice said.

I looked up, my hands still petting the dog. The man was standing about twenty feet in front of me, his hands resting on his hips. He was dressed in a pair of jeans, a flannel shirt, and a hide vest trimmed in lamb's wool. He stood maybe five foot eight and had a medium build. He had a black mustache, black whisker stubble, and dark eyes, his pupils appearing black as well.

"Can I help you?" the man asked.

"I wasn't sure where I could find someone." I stood, my hands to my sides.

"At this time of day you're lucky if you find anyone. Who are you looking for?"

"My dad used to work here," I said.

The man's jaw slid forward before he said his next words. His brow pinched slightly in the middle. "You Sommer's kid?" he asked.

I nodded. He walked closer, extending his hand. "Owen McCormack."

"Genesis," I said. "My dad told me about you."

"He was a good guy to have around. Me and him go way back."

"That's what he said."

"It's a shame," he said. "What happened to him. I'm real sorry."

I looked around. Pictured my dad sitting at one of the long tables. "I guess this is where the men eat," I said.

Owen's eyes followed mine. "Yep. In the mornings they start coming in around four. Most of them want some breakfast, some of them just get coffee. They'll make their lunches over there." Owen pointed to the long counter in front of two refrigerators. "I do the shopping. Keep the place stocked with all kinds of lunch meat, sandwich stuff, you know. Don't see them again until sometime after five. Dinner's at six."

"Did my dad eat breakfast?" I asked. I wanted to picture my dad as if I was accompanying him through an entire day. I wanted to know exactly how he had lived. I wanted to capture all of the things I had missed.

"No, not usually. He'd grab some coffee. Maybe an apple or a granola bar, you know, some kind of snack. He'd be one of the first ones out. Him and a couple of the Canadians."

Just standing on the floor where my dad had stood, breathing the very air that he'd survived on for most of his last twenty years, fascinated me.

"You want to see where the men stay?"

I wanted to see where my dad had slept. I had a feeling Owen understood this. "You don't mind showing me around?"

"Not at all."

I followed Owen outside. Boozer trotted beside us. The trailers were no more than fifty feet apart.

Three wooden steps, whitewashed with the dry residue of salt, led up to the metal door. Inside the trailer, I immediately smelled the generator heat, like burning copper, the cheap varnished paneling, the odor of men, almost familiar, like the scent that something made of iron leaves on the hands, mixed with a hint of wood smoke and something close to kitchen grease.

"These are the rooms," Owen said. "Ten rooms in each trailer. Two bunks to a room."

We were standing in a narrow hallway just to the left of where we had entered, and along the left side of that hallway were five small rooms.

"We've got the shower room in the middle. The rest of the rooms are on the other side of the showers."

I stood in the doorway of the first room. A twin bed ran perpendicular to each of my shoulders. On a trunk at the foot of one of the beds was a nine-inch TV. An orange sleeping bag and pillow lay on top of one of the bed's mattresses. Rumpled sheets and blankets lay on the other. Above both beds were posters of scantily clothed women.

"You want to see where your dad slept?" Owen asked. His voice had turned somber.

My head moved slowly, bringing my chin downward, barely a nod, more of an acknowledgment to his question.

We continued down the hall to the last room on the left. My father had been missing for almost two months. He had not been replaced. His belongings remained intact. He'd slept in a sleeping bag. I didn't know that until I saw his bed. A large blue sleeping bag with a plaid flannel lining. He used two pillows, both cased with old pillowcases we no longer used at home, Ninja Turtles and Power Rangers from when I was small. The same ones I'd used on my bed.

I smiled when I saw them, and chuckled, a laugh not much more than a breath.

"Go on in," Owen said.

And so I did. I walked over to my father's bed, pressed my palm on his sleeping bag, sat on the thin mattress, the bed's springs squeaking beneath my weight. On the wall beside his bed was a poster from a GMC catalog of an extended-cab Sierra. My dad had wanted a new truck.

Below that were four photographs. One was of my dad and me after a snowmobile race when I was no more than five or six. The twins' recent school pictures made up two others. And the last photo was one of Perry and my dad from when they were teenagers. It was summer. They were standing bare chested, their arms around each other's shoulders. Perry was shorter. Both of them appeared tan and lean. Behind them was the lake, so vast, it might as well have been an ocean. But I recognized the color, the green-blue of the fresh water, recognized the bank where they stood, the rocky shoreline and pier near the boat launch at Otter Cove.

There weren't any pictures of Linda.

"You can take them if you'd like," Owen said. He walked into the room and sat on the twin bed across from me. Boozer followed him and lay by his feet.

I didn't want to take the pictures. What I understood then was that my life had felt like pieces of furniture that had been carefully arranged, and one by one those pieces were being moved. I didn't want to move any more of the pieces, as if by changing the arrangement, I might be affecting the outcome of my father's life.

I met Owen's eyes. He blinked slowly, nodded his head. He wasn't going to make me take my father's things. I wouldn't be required to disturb my father's past. I knew as well as anyone that eventually the camp would hire someone new. That another man would be sleeping on my dad's bunk. But I didn't have to be part of that, nor would I be there when it happened. I wanted to tell Owen, "Thanks." I wanted to say, "Thanks for waiting until I got here." I was thankful that my dad had not been replaced before I'd come.

"It must have been a long drive up here for you. You want something to eat?" Owen asked.

"I would," I said. "But could I sit here a little longer?"

"Sure," Owen said. "I'll be over in the kitchen. I'll put on some coffee."

He and Boozer left. I remained on my father's bed, looking at his belongings—the photographs, the sleeping bag, the cartoon pillowcases. My dad didn't have a TV in his room, or a radio. He didn't have a trunk, either. He'd always bring a large duffel bag with him to and from work.

I lay back on the bed, staring up at the ceiling. Paper crinkled beneath my head. I sat up and lifted the pillows. Beneath them were a magazine and a couple of books. I picked up the magazine first. *North Country Real Estate.* The glossy pages showed properties around northern Maine and northern New Hampshire. Mostly parcels of land and cabins. My dad had talked about buying a place on the water. I hadn't taken him seriously. I wished I could go back to that conversation, press him for more answers, know what he was thinking.

I picked up the books. One was a paperback, *Into Thin Air.* The other was a mystery by Kellerman. I couldn't recall having seen my father read books before. I lifted the pillow to return them, and as I did, I noticed a hair clasp poking out from beneath the edge of the sleeping bag. Linda wore hair clasps. She'd pull her long, strawberry blonde hair into a ponytail and hold it with a large barrette. But Linda had never been to the camp. I picked up the clasp. A couple of hairs were trapped in the hinge. They might have been strawberry blond like Linda's, but they also might have been light brown. I held the clasp closer to the window to catch the light, but I still couldn't tell.

Though I left the photographs, I slipped the hair clasp, the magazine, and the two books, as well, into the deep pockets of my coat. I decided I would read the books. I would look through the magazine. It was the closest I could get to my father. And then there was the clasp, a dulled piece of brown plastic with a metal hinge and a couple of broken strands of a woman's hair.

On my way out I looked at the bunk next to my dad's. Other than a bank calendar on the wall and a dark sleeping bag and white pillow, it was nondescript. I wondered who had shared quarters with my father. Did my dad talk to this man before he fell asleep? Did they work beside each other or eat meals together? I felt something close to jealousy, because someone else knew a side to my dad that the rest of us didn't. But then again my father was a serious, private sort of man. Maybe the person who'd shared his quarters was just as private.

CHAPTER
17

I sat one of the tables in the dining hall. Owen sat across from me. He had made me a roast beef sandwich and poured me a cup of coffee.

"Aren't you going to have anything?" I asked.

"I already ate," he said.

I looked again at the benches by the door, the slippers evenly lined up. "Which ones are my dad's?" I asked.

"I'm not sure. He may have packed his with him."

I continued to stare at the slippers, wondering if I recognized any of them.

"You know, the other guys, they took it pretty hard when they heard about what happened to your dad," Owen said.

"Was he close to any of them?" I asked.

"Workers come and go. I don't know how close they get. They're not really the kind of men to open up, you know what I mean? Each one's here in order to bring another buck home. They'll be out there in all kinds of weather, pushing to get another cord on the trucks. I suppose the cutting crews form some kind of loyalty. But even then, they got different jobs, you know. And the equipment's running, so it's not a time for conversation. You couldn't even hear a guy take a piss. Excuse the language, but that's how it is."

"Who'd my dad work with?" I asked.

"He had a couple of Americans on his team. One of the guys was out of Jay. Another from Millinocket."

Owen ran a hand over his mustache, pulling down on a couple of the long whiskers. "Of course no sooner does a guy get used to one crew, than someone walks off and we got a new hire coming on."

I slipped my hand into my coat pocket, felt the barrette against my palm. "Do you ever hire women?" I asked.

"Not since I've been here," Owen said. "I suppose it could happen." He laughed a little. "You looking for work? They won't hire anyone under twenty-one."

"I'm not looking for work," I said. "I got a job over at the Lazy Moose. You hear of it?"

"Can't say that I have. I don't get down that way. I got family down in Millinocket. I head down there on the weekends, pick up groceries for the lot of these guys."

"Anyone stay up here on the weekends?" I asked.

"A couple of the guys out of Canada take shifts. They get paid extra for making sure the generator stays running. Basically just keeping an eye on things. They don't have wives and kids to get home to."

I picked up the coffee cup, staring over the rim at Owen. "Any women ever come around?" I asked.

He nodded. "Sometimes," he said. "Sometimes one of the men will have a guest over. Some of the wives like to come up from time to time. Stay for a night, then head out in the morning. The men don't seem to make too much fuss over it."

"What about my dad?" I asked. "Did he ever have anyone stay over?" I was looking at Owen straight on, the hair clasp still in my hand.

Owen looked off to the side, then back at me. "No," he said.

I wanted him to say more about the women, but he didn't. I looked around at the bare white walls, listened to the silence that seemed to echo between my own breaths. I tried to imagine the dining hall filled with large, hungry, tired men.

"I'm going to have to start fixing dinner for these guys," he said. "We're having chicken and an apple cake for dessert. You planning on sticking around?"

"No, I should head back. You a good cook?" I asked.

"The men don't complain."

Owen was being friendly enough, but something in his demeanor toward me had changed since I'd asked about the women.

"You make a good sandwich," I said.

Owen smiled. "I'm glad you came up. I've heard a lot about you. You made your dad proud."

"Yeah?"

"Yeah. Real proud," he said.

Again, something awkward settled between us. Owen said I had made my dad proud. To be proud of someone, "real proud," you must first love that person. My father had loved me. I had not just lost someone I loved. I had lost someone who loved me more than anyone might ever love me again. Without my dad, without his love, big and unconditional and proud, I was alone.

I fought hard to hold on to my grief. Did Owen see right through my eyes, into my heart? Perhaps he did. He closed the door to that conversation just as gently as he had opened it. It was in the way he looked at me. The way he pressed his lips together and nodded his head as if in deliberation. And then with a voice just as gentle as the expression on his face, he changed the subject.

"You have any trouble getting up here?"

I swallowed before answering, pushing away the tightening ache in my throat. "Not really," I said. I decided not to tell him about my wrong turn.

"You want a thermos for the road?"

"No, I'm good."

"I'll hold on to your father's things. When you're ready for them, let me know."

"Okay. I will."

That was it. There would be no other exchanges. I knew I wouldn't return to the camp again, nor would Owen be down my way. Maybe Linda would one day inquire into my father's few belongings, but I knew I wouldn't.

I petted Boozer for a long time before leaving, digging my fingers into his thick fur, massaging his neck, as if trying to grasp on to something warm and neutral. As if wanting to believe this dog understood everything going on inside me. He was a separate species in this world up on the mountain. I, too, felt like a separate species in my world.

. . .

I left the camp, glancing only once in the rearview mirror. The sky was still blue, but the wind had begun to blow as it oftentimes did in the afternoon. Fine powder swirled, creating a grainy filter through which I could see the small community housing that had contained so much of my father's life, holding it in a capsule.

I stayed in four-wheel-low as I made my way down the mountain and back onto the Golden Road. Again I was sharing my space with logging rigs with rough-looking men perched on seats high above me. One of the drivers honked his horn. Was he flirting or just claiming his right of way? My dad had talked about how a lot of the drivers, particularly the younger ones, worked stoned. "They're paid by the load," he'd said. The high speeds, long hours, and severe grades on the roads were physically and mentally exhausting. Money and survival drove people, he'd tell me. Now I wondered if my dad had gotten high, too, at least in his early years, to keep himself going. Then I reminded myself that my father was different. He made sense. Yes, that was it. He made sense. Smoking weed wouldn't have made sense to him. Leaving his family wouldn't have made sense either.

My trip seemed shorter heading home. As I turned off the Golden Road to make my way once again through the forest to Kokadjo, I had the sensation of "how did I get here?" My mind had clearly consumed the time. It was almost three thirty. Already the daylight was softening, a pinkish glow against the snowfall. About a half mile along the trail, blood appeared in the middle of the tire tracks, at least a foot in diameter. The blood trail continued. A truck had no doubt passed before me, hit a small animal, maybe a fox, and then dragged it for the next hundred feet or so. I thought I would eventually see a corpse, especially once the blood trail stopped, but I never did. Another animal must have already carried it off.

More time passed, at least a half hour. I was once again at the crest of the hill that I had climbed earlier in the day before having taken the wrong trail. I eased my way onto the downward slope slowly, touching the brakes a time or two to maintain control, but not wanting to slow to the point that I would not have the momentum to make it across the gully and up the other hill.

My wheels began to lock and glide over the trail's surface. There wasn't enough friction between the tires and the snow. Then I hit the gully, the frozen stream I had slid over earlier, only the afternoon sun had warmed the icy channel, turning it to slush. My wheels sunk, spinning out against the soft bottom. I tried to rock the truck back and forth, but it was no use. With each effort I only dug myself deeper into the gully.

I stepped out, my boots sinking up to six inches in the mush. The layer at the bottom of the gully felt like mud, creating a vacuum. I climbed back into the cab. The sun seemed to be accelerating in its descent. Daylight was fading quickly.

My dad had traveled this route, as had others. He'd driven the same truck as me. Had he ever become stuck in this same spot? If I had a shovel, I could bail the water out of the divots, scrape the gully free of the slush and bilge. There had to be a cup in the truck somewhere. I had no other strategies. Besides, staying active would keep me warm. I crouched onto the floor and reached under the seat. I found a small cup from a convenience store in town. It still smelled of coffee, reminding me of the morning my dad had given me a ride to Perry's garage. The last morning before he disappeared. That same smell. Had he stopped for coffee before heading out on the lake? Was this the cup he'd drunk from? Probably not, I told myself.

I opened the door, stepped into the gully, then crouched over and began the process of filling cupfuls of the icy muck and throwing the contents into the trees behind me—one cupful after another. I hoped for quick gain, but saw none. It appeared as if the land was leaking fluid at the same rate that I was emptying the crevice. I scooped faster, changing hands from time to time to keep the blood moving in both arms. My back was aching and my legs stiffening. If I crouched any lower, supported my weight onto my heels, I would submerge my hips into the water. Instead, I stood at intervals, stretched out my spine, unlocked my knees, before resuming the process all over again.

I canvassed the happenings of my day as I worked, thought of Owen, of my father's bunk, of the hair clasp I'd found. Surely it had belonged to Linda. It might even have gotten mixed up with the laundry or the pillowcase Dad had brought from home. I thought of all of the men my dad worked with, of the countless hours my dad had spent in the woods—twenty-two years, longer than anyone else at the camp, except for the cook. Owen had said that the other men had taken it hard, what happened to my dad. There it was again, that phrase—"what happened to my dad"—vague because no one could say specifically what had happened, and then there was the awful possibility that we would never know. They'd *taken it hard*. I thought of those words. What did they mean, exactly? The crew my father worked with didn't really open up. New hires came and went. The men were too tired to talk at night, and during the day the machines were running. The guys at the camp didn't really know

{ 194 }

my dad. Maybe it was only then that I understood grief in a different way. Perhaps for most people it meant the same thing as fear. The news of my father had hit them hard not so much over the loss of him, but because they knew whatever had happened to my dad could just as easily happen to them.

Real grief was different. I should know, as it had become the measured beat that moved me through each day. And I knew it would keep something about my father, his presence, alive no matter what. The pain might ease one day, though at the moment I wasn't sure of that, but his memory would always be there, triggered by the smallest of happenings, like the sound of a snowmobile starting, or an empty cup that smelled of old coffee.

And yet, in some ways I wasn't so different from those men. I had attended Christine Bédard's funeral. I had thought, this could have been me. I'd been reminded of her death each time I had driven on the lake. And as I sat through Christine's funeral and my heart ached for her family, I promised myself I would be more careful. I would check the depth of the ice cover before I stepped onto the lake again. I did for a while. But over time, I forgot.

These were my thoughts as I methodically scooped the ice and slush, the precipitation that was beginning to congeal from the dropping temperatures. Dusk had almost passed. Only a sliver of light remained. I heard noise just ahead, then the breaking of a branch, another, the footsteps made by large game. A moose appeared almost like an apparition out of the filtered light and darkness and shadows—a bull moose standing perpendicular to the trail about fifty feet in front of me. "Remain still when you see a moose," my dad had told me. "If you keep still, it won't bother you, unless it's a cow moose that's protecting her young." I was facing a bull that was traveling alone, as the male moose were known to do. I remained motionless, crouched over the gully, the cup suspended inches from the surface. I gauged the animal's size, trying to discern the tines in his antlers. He was a mature male, as large as a small gelding. I didn't know much about horses, but from where I was crouched, I was sure the moose in front of me was that large. He looked strong and powerful and kind, and mysterious in a way that made me wish he would stay there, watch over me, like some kind of messenger from the wild. But I was also more practical than that. A moose could be mean, charge a vehicle, charge a person up a tree. I would remain still and just maybe he would respect me in the same way I felt respect for him.

Something startled him. He stomped one of his front hooves, snorted, raised his head, walked stealthily across the trail, and disappeared into the trees along the other side. I made out a rumbling engine several seconds later. The moose had no doubt heard the oncoming vehicle before me. I stood, climbed back into the truck, turned on the lights, even pressed in the hazard button to give the person who was approaching plenty of warning.

After a few seconds, I decided it was best to stand off a fair distance from my vehicle, just in case the approaching truck wouldn't be able to stop. I stood along a line of trees to the side of the road. A couple more minutes passed before headlights became visible and the rig began to descend the hill toward me, snapping spruce branches in its slow wake. The driver eased onto his brakes a number of times and shifted to lower gears. He was approaching at no more than three to five miles an hour. He slowed to a stop at least fifty feet from my truck. He was driving a tanker rig, not a logging trailer. He was no doubt one of the delivery carriers hauling propane to the different camps.

I listened as he engaged his emergency brake, heard him shift his truck to neutral. His door opened. He stepped out, the trail's surface crunching beneath his feet. He took several steps away from his cab, the diesel engine still clattering away. "Hell of a place to get stuck," he yelled.

For the most part he looked like a shadow because of the glare of his headlights from behind him. Then he moved forward, making slow, easy strides toward me. My stomach tightened. It was the same flannel shirt, the same build, the same man who had noticed me at the restaurant in Kokadjo almost twelve hours before.

CHAPTER
18

"We got a couple of options," the man said. "I've got a come-along winch in my cab. I could fasten it to one of the trees up ahead and try and pull you out. Or, I could line my vehicle up behind yours and push you till you're on your way. Of course, my fender could scrape your tailgate a little."

"What do you suggest?" I asked.

"My rig's got enough weight where pushing you out's going to be the easiest. That is, if you're not too worried about your truck getting scratched."

"I'm not worried about my truck," I said.

Here I was standing in the middle of nowhere. Even if I screamed, the wind would devour the sound, not to mention there wasn't another living soul to hear me other than this stranger and the wildlife. Darkness had already consumed every bit of natural light. And it was cold. I might not make it till morning on my own. I had no choice. I'd have to trust this man.

The man walked around my truck as if he was inspecting it. He even dragged a hand along the tailgate. Then he looked at me, looked at me long and hard. My calf muscles stiffened.

"This truck looks familiar," he said. "Is this Mike Sommer's?"

He knew my dad, and I thought that was a good thing, so I said, "Yes."

"Geez, you must be his kid. I thought I recognized you." He stepped forward and extended his hand. "Wayne Snell," he said. "I've known your dad for years."

He wasn't speaking in the past tense, meaning, he didn't say, "I *knew* your dad for years," or "Didn't this truck *used to* belong to Mike?" And why did he recognize me? I felt my mind shoveling thoughts around, as if trying to find a place to fit them.

"I've seen your picture," he said. "Your dad used to show me photos of his kids. You're the one who races, right?"

My dad must have trusted this man if he'd shown him pictures of Scott and Alex and me. And he'd told him I raced. Had my father kept pictures of us in his wallet? I hadn't noticed, had never paid attention when he'd taken out his wallet to pay for things.

"Were you friends?" I asked.

"Yeah, I guess you could say that," Wayne said. "We go way back, you know. I was driving trucks back when

Mike worked for the outfit over in Jay, when he was at the contractor camp."

Wayne was a trucker. Maybe he didn't know about what had happened to my dad. Was I supposed to break the news?

"Did you hear?" I asked.

And then he stopped talking. His head tipped up and down slowly. He *had* heard.

"Word's been getting around," he said. "It's a real shame."

"Anybody have any ideas about what might have happened to him?" I asked.

"He could have had engine trouble. The boat could have bucked when he tried to start it, sent him over. There was a storm that day. He could have lost his balance."

"It seems weird though," I said. "He's been out on boats his whole life."

"I know what you're saying, but it happens," Wayne said.

"Can I ask you something?"

"Sure."

"Are there any women up this way that my dad might have known?" My hands were shoved into my pockets, my right hand fingering the hair clasp that I'd found earlier. God, how I wanted answers.

"Your dad's been up here so long, he probably knew a lot of the folks working up here. There's a couple of women who drive trucks for the companies. There's some other women who work at the mills and sometimes come up this way."

"Anyone you can think of that my dad might have known well?"

If someone would just tell me about my dad, tell me everything I didn't know, then I could go home and soak in the tub until the water turned cold. I could eat a frozen pizza and read a book and fall asleep. Yes, that was what I wanted. Then I remembered Gabe. I would never make it back for dinner.

Wayne didn't answer right away. I tried to read his expression, but it was dark, and I wasn't sure what anything on his face might mean. Maybe he was surprised by my question, or maybe he was simply trying to recall any women my dad might have known.

"There was one woman," he said. "I'd seen your dad with her a couple of times at the camp. I think she drove a truck for one of the mills."

An odd feeling of relief settled in my stomach. "Do you know who she was? Where I could find her?"

"I'm not sure."

"Anyone else who might know?" I asked.

"Your guess is as good as mine," he said. "Like I said, I only saw her a couple of times."

"What did she look like?" I asked.

"She had long brown hair. She looked around forty. That's all I remember."

I changed the questions. "Do you know a guy by the name of Marc Suter?" I asked.

"Marc? Oh, yeah, I know Suter. Been around longer than your dad."

"You know where I could find him?"

"Sure. Seen him down in Millinocket not too long ago. Making deliveries for a lumber mill down there. A place called Devereaux Timber. Small operation."

"Does he live down there?" I asked.

"Can't answer to that, but I *do* know he was at the job no more than a month ago."

Wayne didn't ask the reason for my questions. Either it didn't occur to him to ask, or else he didn't consider it any of his business. I was glad.

"How about we get you on your way home," he said. "Why don't you climb in and shift your truck to neutral. Don't put it in drive till we've got you the rest of the way up the hill."

"Sounds good," I said.

He remained where he was. "Well, daughter of Mike Sommer, it was nice to meet you."

I offered him my hand. "I'm Genesis," I said. "Thanks for the help."

He shook my hand. Then he turned toward the glow of his headlights and walked back to his cab.

I climbed into my truck and followed his instructions. Very smoothly he lined his rig up behind my tailgate. I heard the metal scrape. I didn't care. Soon I felt a slight jolt, then a surge as my vehicle was pushed out of the ice and mush, out of the gully and onto the incline. From there we moved steadily up the hill. At the top, Wayne must have braked, for my truck stopped moving. I shifted to drive and pressed on the gas. The tires immediately picked up traction.

Wayne stayed behind me the rest of the way to Kokadjo, his lights helping me to steer along the frozen tracks on the trail. At the store I turned right toward Sebaticuk. Wayne made a left, honking his horn a couple of times after the turn.

I thought of my conversation with Wayne. Maybe there *had* been another woman in my dad's life. If there was any chance my dad was alive, I had to know. I would try and find Marc Suter. I was certain he'd be able to put me in touch with the woman Wayne had mentioned.

I looked at my watch. Almost seven. I had no way of calling Gabe and telling him I couldn't make it. I wondered if he'd wait.

CHAPTER 19

It was almost seven thirty by the time I got back to town. Instead of turning left toward the house, I continued down Main Street, toward Kelly's Landing, an inn and restaurant that overlooked the lake. There were only a handful of vehicles in the parking lot. I didn't know if any of them belonged to Gabe but felt fairly certain he would have given up on me. I checked my face in the rearview mirror just in case. I could have definitely used a shower. I pulled my hat down lower to cover my dingy hair. Was I hoping he'd still be there?

As I approached the restaurant, the door opened. Gabe was on his way out, wearing his heavy green parka and a gray knit cap. I smiled big, feeling very glad to see him.

"Hey," he said with surprise. "I didn't think you'd show."

"I wasn't sure I would either. Something came up. I'm really sorry."

"Everything okay? You want to go in and get something to eat?"

"I'm not really hungry," I said. "I would have called but I don't have a cell. Besides, I wouldn't have known how to reach you."

We were standing beneath the porch light of the restaurant, the vast expanse of lake before us, and so much snow.

Gabe looked around as if trying to decide what to do next. "Do you want to go for a walk?" he asked.

I'd been in the cold all day, and yet suddenly I *did* want to go for a walk. "Okay," I said.

"Come on." He started walking. I followed him down the bank from the landing, stepped onto the frozen surface of the water, the cold punctuating every sound, the dry crunching of our feet against the snow, the brushing of our coat sleeves against our sides, our breathing.

"How's your job going?" I asked.

"Pretty good."

"Do you like what you do?"

"Yeah, for the most part. I'd thought at one time about being a doctor, but I like being outside. I like the wildlife. What about you?" he asked.

"I guess I haven't had a lot of time to think about it. Things are sort of different for me."

Did I want to reveal more? Did I suddenly want to trust this person beside me who might as well have been a complete stranger? My life *was* different from Gabe's, and yet I didn't want that difference to define me. I wanted to say, "but that's not who I am." I wanted possibilities. I wanted to go to college or I didn't want to go to college, but I wanted there to be a choice. I continued to walk beside Gabe, waiting for him to say something. He had turned silent and I wondered if I'd said something wrong.

Gabes's footsteps slowed. His entire body seemed to hesitate. I slowed beside him, waiting through layers of quiet until he finally spoke. "I started my internship right after Christmas. People I work with talked about a man going missing on the lake. I'd heard his name. It wasn't until today that I realized the man was your dad," he said. And then, "Does me bringing this up bother you?"

My jaw had become cold. I felt my words slur as I spoke them. "I don't think so." Gabe's words had come unexpectedly. At first I felt uncomfortable, but then I felt something else going on as well, something loosening inside me. Gabe was neutral, separate from everyone I knew and everything going on around me. I felt as if his very presence, combined with the cold glow of the moonlight on the lake, was softening my anger and rigidity. "It's been a long day," I said.

"Do you want to talk about it?"

Up until that point I had wanted to keep my grief private and pure. I'd barely talked about it with Mémère or Perry or Linda and the twins. Too much sadness lingered between us. With others I'd avoided the subject for different reasons, mostly ones that had to do with my privacy and their discomfort. My vulnerability made others uncomfortable. Was it because they had known my father too? Was it easier with Gabe because he was a stranger? "I don't mind," I told him.

Gabe seemed to proceed cautiously, his words matching his slow steps. "So you said it's been a long day. What happened?" he asked.

I felt as if the cold air was crystallizing inside my lungs, and then when I expelled it, a sound came out, a forced laugh, abrupt and not real. "Oh, geez, where do I start?" I took another long breath, and then I told him about driving up to the logging camp to see where my dad had worked.

"You'd never been up there before?" Gabe asked.

"No. Is that weird? I mean, I guess that sounds weird, doesn't it?"

"Maybe not so weird. How long had he worked up there?"

"All my life, at one camp or another. He'd come home for long weekends. I don't know why we never went up there. I guess no one really thought about it."

"But you went *now*," Gabe said, as if trying to ease whatever guilt I was feeling.

"Yeah, I did."

I knew I'd gone up to the camp to find out if my dad was having an affair. To find out if he might still be alive. But perhaps I'd driven up there for other reasons as well. "I wanted to know his day," I told Gabe. "Where he ate, where he slept. I wanted to understand what he did. It's not an easy drive up there. The trails aren't groomed or anything. And he made that trip every week."

"Did you have any trouble making the drive?"

"Going up wasn't too bad, other than a wrong turn. But coming back, the snow and ice had softened. I got stuck at one point. I was probably there for a couple of hours before this guy came up behind me. He pushed me out with his truck."

"And you don't have a cell phone?" Gabe asked.

"No. I used to. I don't think there's a signal where I was anyway. You can usually pick up a signal at the camp, but it's not always very strong. Calls get lost."

I thought about all the times my dad had contacted us from camp with his cell phone, all the sentences that had gotten lost somewhere when the connection was broken, all the words I had never heard. And then there were all those years when my father hadn't had a cell phone. When he, along with the other men, had to share the camp's radio telephone.

"You're pretty brave for going up there. I've got a couple of sisters. They never would have gone up there alone. They wouldn't be racing cars, either."

It was interesting to learn about someone else, to get out of my own situation for a while. I liked the curiosity I felt with Gabe.

"What are they like?" I asked.

"Jess is ten. She's a half sister. She's okay, but she's afraid of the dark and just about anything else a person can be afraid of. She shares a room with Marguerite, my other sister."

"How old is she?"

"Sixteen."

"What's she like?" I asked.

"She's not too bad. Sometimes I actually think we're pretty close. It all depends on her mood or who she's going out with."

We were walking parallel to the shore now, about sixty feet out.

"What about you?" he asked. "You have any brothers or sisters?"

So I told him about the twins. "It's not easy with my dad gone. Sometimes I'm not sure Linda knows what to do with them. Maybe she'd be better with girls."

"Is Linda your mom?"

"My stepmom," I said. "My mom left when I was six."

"So did my dad. I was seven."

"No way," I said. "So we have more in common than just the ice."

"I guess so."

"Do you see him? Your father?" I asked.

"I used to. On weekends. Not so much anymore. What about you? Do you see your mom?"

"Only once," I told him. "She doesn't live here."

"How old were you when you saw her?"

"Ten. My dad wanted to take us all to Florida. He wanted to show us Disney World. My mom works at the airport in Portland. She rents cars. My dad seemed to think it would be a good thing if we saw each other. I'm not so sure that was the real reason though. Maybe *he* wanted to see her, to show her how well we were doing, how well he was doing with her gone. So he walked me over to her counter. She was there. It was really awkward."

"That's too bad. Sometimes that's how I feel with my dad. Like each time we see each other we're two strangers meeting for the first time."

"I'm sorry," I said.

Gabe shrugged his shoulders. "It's okay. No big deal."

"You know what was weird, when I saw my mom? She looked just like me. I mean, older, of course. I didn't like that. I didn't want to look like her. I wanted to look like my dad."

"It sounds like you and your dad were close."

Flashes of my father cut across my mind in no particular order, the two of us bumping along in his truck, or grocery shopping, or his big happy face wet with snow after I'd won a race. "I always knew we were close," I said. "I know it more now. Maybe we love someone more when they're gone. I mean, I would get mad at my dad sometimes. But now that all seems so trivial. I guess we can take someone for granted when they're always there. We become selfish, you know, thinking about our own needs and what we're getting or not getting. I'd get mad sometimes because my dad was away so much, even though he was away working so he could take care of all of us. I remember sulking when I was fourteen because he wouldn't let me go camping with some of the other kids. I thought he didn't trust me. When he left to go up to the logging camp that week, I wouldn't even tell him good-bye. Another time I got mad because he reeled in a fish I'd caught. I'd wanted to do it myself. Now I feel guilty for those things. I want to go back and live my life perfectly. I want to go back and be more forgiving."

I felt like I hadn't talked this much in years. And here Gabe didn't even know me. What was I thinking? But then Gabe's body moved just the slightest bit closer to mine as we walked, and ever so slowly he wrapped his arm over my shoulder. I didn't resist. Instead I eased my weight toward him as if walking with a good friend.

"Maybe you don't love a person more when they're gone," he said. "Maybe you just allow yourself to stop and feel it. I mean, it takes two people going through all kinds of things together, good and bad. So, everything you feel now was always there, and your dad would have known that. If it was perfect or you were perfect all the time, I don't see how that could be love."

"It would all be kind of phony, wouldn't it." My words weren't a question. I knew what he was saying.

"Yeah, I think it would. When we love someone, we're ourselves, you know, flaws and all. We're selfish and we're unselfish. We're good and we're bad. We're all those things. If we weren't, we wouldn't have to try so hard to be better. It's the trying so hard that *does* make us better."

"I can buy that," I said.

"In other words, go easy on yourself, okay?"

"I'll try."

Gabe laughed, a good laugh, hearty and light at the same time. It took me a minute before I'd realized what I'd said.

He squeezed my shoulder. "You cold?" he asked.

"Getting there."

"Me too. Want to turn around and get something warm to drink?"

"That sounds good."

So we turned around. Gabe dropped his arm from my shoulder, allowing us to walk more easily. I'd opened up to him, but I hadn't told him everything, meaning, I hadn't told him about going to the logging camp to follow up on what Eric had said about there being a woman involved. But then again, maybe I *had* told Gabe the real reason I'd made the trip, kind of like the difference between something in my head and in my heart. In my head I was trying to figure things out, trying to prove or disprove that there was a woman. But in my heart, I just wanted to be as close to my father as I could get, and seeing where he worked, understanding his day a little better, gave me a glimpse of him I might otherwise never have had.

CHAPTER
20

It was Gabe who told me the meaning of *surreal*. I worked the late shift on Tuesday, which meant I went in at two and got off at ten, when the restaurant closed. Gabe met me at the end of my shift, and we walked again—this time down Main Street and up to the playground at the school. We brushed off the snow on a couple of swings.

"Thanks for last night," I told him as we each sat in one of the rubber seats.

"For what?"

"For listening."

"You're easy to listen to."

"I can't believe all the things I was saying to you."

"Gen, you've been through a lot. Seriously. You've got to talk to someone. Besides, I like talking with you."

We swung slowly, unsettling the ice in the chains and sending small flecks onto our shoulders.

"I'm glad we met," I said.

Gabe bumped my foot with his. "Me too."

"You know what's weird?"

"What's that?"

"This is the first thing that's felt real since my dad went missing. I mean, nothing else feels natural anymore. I don't know how else to explain it. Like I'm not standing on solid ground. Like I'm here, but I'm not really here."

Was it Gabe's easiness, his very presence that made me talk? Or was it the fact that I couldn't *not* talk anymore?

Gabe was staring at the ground as he listened. "I don't know how you do it," he said. "I mean, you must be on autopilot. Like your body is going through the motions just to keep you moving."

"That's exactly how it feels," I said. "I wake, I eat, but nothing seems familiar." I was looking directly at him, staring at the silhouette of his profile, his deep jawline, his flat chin, his protruding brow.

"It's called *surreal*," he told me. "Where everything seems distorted," he went on.

"How do you *know*?" I asked. "How can you describe everything so exact?"

"It's not like I've been through anything like this. Other than my dad leaving, my life's been pretty normal. I just try to imagine, you know. When you sit out on the ice all day, you get to thinking about things. I wonder what it would feel like to be you. I know that sounds weird, but I start thinking about how it all happened and where you were and the moment you knew something was wrong. I start thinking about how I would feel if I were you. People always say, 'I can't imagine,' when something bad happens to someone. So I *try* to imagine it, and then I think how if I were you, everything would feel surreal, you know. I don't know how you do it. I mean, going up to the camp, and working like you are. Not even being in school. You're strong, Gen."

Gabe's words seemed to devour everything I might have said, because they said it better. I lay my hand on his shoulder, the nylon of my glove scraping against his jacket. He stopped looking at the ground. The night was clear, the moon thin, allowing just enough light for us to see each other.

"You can talk to me," he said.

I hesitated at first. Like the night before, I wasn't sure where to begin. But once I found my words, I talked— really talked, as if I were listening to myself for the first time. "When something like this happens, you're sup- posed to have some warning, right? I mean, you should be able to look back and realize a look or a feeling that you didn't notice at first. I've spent so long looking for the warning. Thinking about the last time I saw my dad, remembering what he said, how he looked. I was looking in the wrong place, the wrong hour, the wrong minute."

Gabe reached up and took hold of my hand, bringing it down to our sides, pulling the two swings closer together.

"Tonight when you were talking, that's when it hit me," I said. "When you were talking about the unfamiliar.

I felt it before my dad went out on the boat. Before we left the house. I was standing in front of the mirror brushing my hair. It was as if I were a stranger looking into a different world. The smells, the objects around me. I remember every detail of that morning."

"And then what happened?" Gabe asked.

"My dad called me to come downstairs. My jacket was hanging on the banister. It wasn't hanging by the back door. I never thought of that until now. I always left my jacket by the door. My dad must have brought it to me, put it on the banister for me. When I put it on, it felt tight, like I was suffocating. I remember that feeling. That's how I feel now. That's how I've felt every day since."

My breathing became shallow as I talked, my chest felt like a spring wound too tight, and an awful denseness pushed its way from my sternum to my throat. Did Gabe hear it in my voice? Could he see the changes in my body in the moonlight? He stood and gently pulled me toward him, wrapped his arms around my shoulders, tucked his chin onto my head. My body went slack—my jaw, my shoulders—and I cried, slow at first, like a small crack, the kind that expands with pressure, that turns into a downright break. I gasped, truly feeling like I couldn't get enough air. I gasped again, louder, more desperate. Then I sobbed. Gabe continued to hold me, grabbed fistfuls of my jacket in his hands. Held me even after my crying finally eased.

"If I had a handkerchief, I'd give it to you," Gabe said.

"No one carries handkerchiefs anymore," I managed to say, though the attempt to talk between my sniffs and gulps of air may very well have sounded pathetic.

"Still, if I had one . . ."

I laughed, cried some more, wrapped my arms around his waist and clasped my hands together against his back.

"You cold?" he asked.

"Yeah."

"Me too. Want to walk some more?"

I didn't really want to walk. I wanted to go home to a warm house with a family and a dog. I wanted to crawl into a warm bed.

"Let me ask you something," Gabe said. "If you could have three wishes, other than your dad being home, what would they be?"

"You go first," I said.

"Turning the question around on me, are you?"

"Well, yeah. I don't want to be the one doing all the talking . . . and crying," I added. "Geez, I'm such a mess." My face was still pressed against his jacket, the canvas in that small spot warm and damp from both my tears and my breath.

Gabe let out a slow, "Hmm." He moved his arms up and down on my back and bounced his outward knee, no doubt trying to regain a little warmth. "A fire, a cup of mulled cider, and some music, maybe Green Day," he finally said.

"That wouldn't be too hard to arrange," I told him.

"No?"

"No. At least the fire and the cider. I can't guarantee the music." I unclasped my hands and stood. "Brrr." I jiggled my arms and legs, trying to shake the stiffness out of them.

"You leading the way?"

"Yeah," I said, reaching for his hand.

We walked back to the Lazy Moose, where both our trucks were parked.

"You want to follow me?" I asked.

"Where are we going?"

"I have a friend on the ski team," I said. "They practice over at Cat Mountain, not much more than ten minutes from here. There's an après-ski with a large fireplace that stays open late, and if I'm not mistaken, there'll be cider there too."

"Do you know what the name Sommer means?" he asked.

What in the world was he talking about? I'm sure my expression said just as much.

"It means 'commander.' Someone who takes charge," he told me.

A low moment followed. My father had called me the commander. He'd say that before I raced.

"How did you know that?" I asked.

"I'm a wealth of pointless trivia. Did you know that the Latin word for 'fisherman' is *piscator*? Or that a whale's heart weighs one ton?"

"Do you sit out on the ice and think up questions, then go home and look them up?"

"More or less."

"What does your name mean?" I asked.

"Hamilton was originally *Hambleton*, from the manor of Hambleton in Buckinghamshire. William, the third son of Robert, third Earl of Leicester, took the surname from the place of his birth. And yes, I'll follow you to the lodge," he said.

I laughed, a real laugh.

"Okay, so, I'll see you up there?" I said.

"I'm right behind you."

I climbed into my truck and started it. From my rearview mirror I watched Gabe walk to the parking space behind me and get into his red Tacoma. So he was a piscator, and a whale's heart weighed a ton, and somewhere in Gabe's family, someone had been English. I pulled out of the parking lot behind the restaurant, the light from Gabe's headlights now behind me.

CHAPTER
21

The drive to the lodge took exactly twelve minutes. Strange. I didn't think about anything other than checking every so often to make sure Gabe was still with me. Perhaps in crying I had settled into something close to exhaustion, a welcome vegetative state in which other than the sound of the truck's engine, the feel of the steering wheel beneath my hands, and the glow of Gabe's headlights behind me, there was nothing else to notice. This was different than just going through the motions. This was something close to liberation. For the first time in nearly two months, I didn't feel like I was struggling just to breathe.

About ten vehicles were parked outside the lodge when we got there. I checked my watch. It was a little after ten thirty. Inside the log building was a large stone fireplace; however, most of the customers were gathered at the bar. A few others were sitting at tables. Country music was playing instead of Green Day. Something by Martina McBride. It would have to do. Two bartenders were working. Both of them women. I recognized one as the woman Perry had been with at Woody's after the races. She was busy talking with a customer and didn't see us.

There was a sofa and a couple of chairs around the fireplace, all of them empty.

"Want to have a seat?" Gabe asked. "And I'll get us something to drink?"

"That sounds good," I said.

So I sat on the sofa while Gabe walked over to the bar. The fire had recently been stoked. The flames were large and warm, the heat slightly stinging the raw skin around my eyes. When had I ever cried so much? And yet I felt no apologies for it. I wasn't trying to impress Gabe. That's what struck me the most. It wasn't that I wasn't interested in him. I simply didn't have it in me to put on a show, and something about him didn't require it. And so I breathed in deeply, exhaled deeply, and sank back into the warm leather, my body completely relaxed. I could sleep. I could fall asleep and maybe nobody would even notice I was there. I began to doze. Began to dream about something that made no sense. About Hillary Clinton approaching a podium, about to give a speech, and Annie and me standing in the audience, and even in the dream, I wondered why I was having such a dream. Then I was awakened. Not by Gabe but by Perry.

"I thought that was you."

When I opened my eyes, he was standing in front of

me. Beside him was Gabe, holding two mugs of hot cider. He handed one to me. I cradled my fingers around it and held it close to my face, feeling my skin moisten from the steam.

"What are you doing here?" I asked Perry. Then I remembered the woman at the bar. "That's right," I said, before he answered. "I saw your friend." I was still sitting back against the sofa. "Perry, this is Gabe. Gabe, this is Perry." My voice was as mellow as the rest of me. I wasn't ready to relinquish my newfound state of vegetative peace.

"We already met," Perry said. "I saw the two of you walk in and introduced myself."

Perry sat down on one side of me. Gabe sat down on the other. "Good to see you out," Perry said.

"I go out," I told him.

Perry's laugh had a sarcastic edge.

"Yeah, whatever," I said.

"You talk to Linda?" he asked.

"I saw her this morning. Why?"

"Just wondering." He leaned back next to me, stretched out his legs in front of him, and clasped his hands together over his stomach.

"Wondering about what?" I asked. "What's up?"

"She called me this afternoon. I was just closing up the garage, about to head out."

"What'd she want?"

"Wanted to talk. She was all upset, crying. I could

barely understand her, so I told her I'd be over. She said the boys were there, and could she come over to the garage and talk."

Gabe leaned forward. "You know I can go wait over by the bar if you guys need to talk. Seriously, I don't mind."

Perry waved a hand toward him, dismissing what he'd said. "No need to go anywhere," he said. "Just family stuff."

"So did she come over to the garage?" I asked.

"Yeah, she came over. We sat back in my office and talked. She said she wasn't going to stay long, that the boys were at the house. She wanted to talk about Mike. Said the week before he'd left to go out on the lake that they'd gone into town. Stopped over at Kelly's Landing to get a bite to eat. She said they'd gotten into a fight."

"Her and Dad?" I couldn't believe it. I'd never even heard my dad and Linda disagree about anything. "Did she tell you what it was about?" I asked.

"She said she'd been on him about getting a job around here. Not being gone so much."

"Getting a job *where?*" I asked.

Perry rubbed a hand over his face. "I don't know. I guess she had some ideas."

"That's what they fought over?"

Gabe stood. I'd almost forgotten he was there. "I'll be right back," he said.

"I think it had more to do with Mike wanting to stay

{ 223 }

on at the camp so he could buy a place on the water. Said the pay was better and he could put in extra hours there."

I wondered if that was the only reason my dad wanted to stay on at the camp. Still, I came to my father's defense. "That's nothing to fight over," I said.

"How many things are?"

"Are what? Worth fighting over?"

"Yeah."

"I don't know."

"My point exactly."

"Is that why you never married?" I asked.

"That's part of it."

"What's the other part?" I asked.

"I'll tell you when I find out."

I leaned my head on his shoulder, still feeling tired, still wanting to sleep. "So that was it?" I asked. "That's what Linda wanted to talk to you about?"

"She feels bad," Perry said. "Feels bad she got mad at him. She'd told him if he loved her he'd be more concerned about being home than about a house on the lake. The next day he left for the company camp."

I closed my eyes, and as I sat there, I started thinking about how my dad was the night before he'd disappeared. He usually drove home from the camp each Thursday night. That week he'd signed on to work Friday, which the men were allowed to do if they wanted to get in some extra hours. I'd headed over to the Lazy

Moose straight from school. By the time I'd gotten home, my dad and Linda and the twins were already in bed. I hadn't seen my father until the next morning.

"Linda shouldn't beat herself up over this. Nobody's perfect," I said, thinking back on my conversation with Gabe.

"What do you think Mike would be telling her right now?" Perry asked.

"To go easy on herself."

"Yeah."

"And to let the twins watch me race." I opened my eyes.

"You still hung up on that?"

"Of course I am," I looked over to the bar. I saw Gabe standing off by himself, still holding his mug of cider.

"Seems like a nice guy," Perry said, following my gaze.

"Yeah."

"Where'd you two meet?"

I smiled. "On the ice."

"What, was he at one of the races or something?"

"Something like that," I said.

A couple of seconds passed between us, both of us looking toward Gabe. Then Perry asked, "What's your schedule like this week?"

"Late shift tomorrow and Wednesday. Thursday off."

"What time do you go in?"

"One. Why?"

"What about Linda?" Perry asked.

"She leaves the house around two. Why all the questions?"

"I could take some time off tomorrow morning. What about we take Linda out for a little spin?"

"Take her out on the ice?"

"Yeah."

I let the idea sink in, and as it sank in, I liked it. "There's one problem."

"What's that?"

"She won't go," I said.

"We won't tell her where we're taking her. She's got to see what it's all about. See how safe it is. She'll be hooked."

"How are we going to get her there?"

"I'm going to pick you two up for breakfast in the morning. I'll already have the car out on the ice. It'll work. Trust me."

I looked at Perry. His lustrous black hair was beginning to gray, and there was a weight beneath his eyes and along his jawline I hadn't noticed before.

"What time?" I asked.

"I'll be there at nine."

"Deal," I said.

CHAPTER

22

We were crawling to a better position. Not running to it. Not even walking. But crawling, pulling ourselves inch by inch to higher ground so that we might have a better view, a better understanding of everything happening to us. That's how I felt on that Wednesday morning when Perry showed up. The twins had already left for school. I dressed warm, knowing we were going to be on the lake, and encouraged Linda to do the same.

"It's cold out there," I'd said. "Better bundle up."

And it *was* cold. Barely above zero.

Linda thought we were going to breakfast. Still, I knew she was wearing thermals. Could tell by the way her jeans fit. She also wore her hat and scarf and her long down jacket.

Perry was driving his Blazer. Linda and I met him in the driveway. In the front seat he had a bag from Millie's Bakery and a cardboard beverage container holding three coffees.

"I thought we were going *out* to breakfast," Linda said.

"We *are* going out." Perry had a loopy grin on his face.

I sat in the backseat, observing their exchanges.

"Perry Sommer, what are you up to?" Linda asked.

Perry had already backed out of the driveway and was heading toward town.

"Just trust me," he said.

Then Linda turned around in her seat. "Did you know about this?" she asked me.

"Know about what?"

She released a rumbling sigh as she sank back against the seat. No one spoke again until Perry turned off at Wharf Junction and started heading out onto the lake.

"What are you doing?" Linda demanded. "Where are you taking me?"

Did I detect an edge of adrenaline? Or was she really pissed off? She was now sitting sideways in her seat, facing Perry. Up ahead was my car, a dab of blue in a fog of blowing snow.

"Where's your sense of adventure?" Perry answered her.

"What are you scheming?"

"I'm not scheming anything." The grin on Perry's face had now doubled in size.

The stretch of plowed road over the lake toward my car was nearly the size of a football field. The wind was gaining momentum against the vehicle, howling through the vents and against the windows the farther we drove away from shore.

"Perry, turn around," Linda said. Whatever thrill I

might have detected in her voice was gone. She now sounded purely terrified.

"You ever been on the ice?" Perry asked her.

"Perry, I said turn around."

Perry ignored her. From where I was sitting, I could see Linda's hand grip the armrest on the passenger door.

"The ice is four feet deep here," I told her. "No different from driving across a sturdy bridge."

She didn't say anything. Her head and shoulders remained fixed in place, pressed solidly against the headrest and seat.

Perry parked his Blazer alongside my car and the empty trailer. He looked at Linda as he shut off his engine. "You won't let the twins watch Gen race. Hell, you won't even let them out on the ice. Why?" he asked firmly.

"They're not your kids," Linda said.

"No, but they're my nephews. And they're Gen's brothers."

Perry was being hard on Linda, and I felt sure he was going to make her cry. For a second I wanted to tell him to stop, to turn around and take Linda home. Maybe what we were doing was wrong.

Perry handed each of us a coffee. He turned in his seat so that his back was against the driver's side door. "I want to tell you something," he said, again speaking to Linda. "I want to tell you something about Mike and me."

From what I could see of the back of Linda's head, she was staring forward. Maybe she was mad. Or maybe she was trying not to cry. Nonetheless, she didn't discourage Perry from continuing, so he did.

"Mike wasn't afraid of anything. When our dad put us on a snowmobile and pointed the machine down a hill, Mike drove it down the hill, and then he drove it up another. Me, I was scared shitless, afraid I would fall off. And I *did* fall off. As soon as Mike started to climb the hill, I flew off the back. The machine turned sideways, not having enough momentum for the climb, and Mike, he went flying off too. But he got up, ran through the snow, took hold of the machine as it was still running, set it up right, and climbed back on. He yelled at me to come on, so, I climbed back on too. Same thing when he was playing football. He was a linebacker. He'd take a tackle hard, and he'd get right back up and keep on playing. Played with a sprained ankle once. Dislocated his shoulder another time, and kept playing with that, too. Sometimes that's what you've got to do, Linda. You've gotten knocked down. You've gotten knocked down hard. But you got to get up. You can't let this ice, or this lake, or anything else stop you. And you can't let your fear get in the way of the twins. It's not natural."

Linda didn't respond at first—didn't move, didn't say anything. And so we waited. Enough had already been said. I sipped my coffee. Perry did the same. Linda was holding hers over her left knee.

"So what do you have in mind?" she finally asked, her voice as calm and quiet as a small ember about to go out.

"We're going to take you out on the track. We're going to let you see how it feels."

"Perry, I can't do that," Linda said. "Isn't just being out here enough?"

"Like I said earlier, what are you afraid of?"

Linda's head sank forward, like something was collapsing inside of her. "I don't know," she said. "Everything, I guess. Afraid of being alone, afraid of falling through the ice. Afraid of not being needed anymore."

Perry reached over and laid his hand on her shoulder. "Look, we'll take the car out on the track, drive it slowly, let you get used to it."

This time Linda didn't resist. Though she didn't say anything, her head gave the slightest nod forward.

We drank our coffee; we each ate a Danish. Then we ducked into our coats and scarves and braced ourselves against the wind and cold.

"You ever been on the ice?" Perry asked her for the second time.

"I used to ice-skate on a pond," Linda told him. "That was back in New Hampshire."

"Who's driving?" I asked Perry.

He reached inside my Mustang for my helmet, handed it to me, and said, "You are."

I tried to read Linda's expression. Was it one of anticipation? Worry?

She looked out over the lake. "It's hard to believe there's so much water beneath us," she said.

Did the thought cross her mind that Dad might be beneath us too? I'm sure it did. Since his disappearance, so many things had seemed to hang between us, as if our thoughts were curtains each of us could see, though dared not acknowledge or draw aside.

Perry brought his snowmobile helmet out of the back of his Blazer. Instead of handing it to her, he removed her knit cap and pulled the helmet down over her head.

"You've been on a snowmobile before, haven't you?" he asked her.

"Yes," she said.

"Just picture yourself riding a snowmobile. Don't even think about being on the lake," he told her.

Perry handed me the keys. "It's all yours, Little Bit."

And so I climbed into the driver's side of the Mustang while Linda walked around the car and opened the passenger door.

"Can you see?" she asked me.

The wind was stirring up snow phantoms. Nothing I wasn't used to. "I can see." I secured my harness straps and pulled my visor down over my face. Beside me, Linda strapped herself in.

"You okay?" I asked her.

"Maybe if I lie I'll feel better," she said. "Sure, I'm fine."

I started the engine, drove the car around Perry's vehicle and toward the track.

"How fast do you go?" Linda asked. She was practically yelling to be heard over the car's rumble and the wind whipping through the bare windows and open back.

"It depends on the weather and who I'm racing against. We won't go fast today."

"I see you're avoiding the question."

That was good, I thought. A little sarcasm.

Once on the track I brought up the speed to fifteen miles an hour, then twenty. I leveled off at thirty. Linda leaned over to read the speedometer.

"How fast do you have to go to win a race?" she asked.

So she was trying her question out a different way, and I debated about whether to give her an honest answer. "Are you going to stay in the car if I tell you?"

"Unless you stop, it doesn't look like I have much choice."

Perry waved to us as we rounded the corner of our first lap.

"I could show you," I told her, testing the waters.

I was now approaching the first curve of the second lap.

"This feels different than riding on the road," Linda said.

"How so?"

"It reminds me of when I was skating as a child. Like we're gliding."

"That's because there's not as much traction," I told her.

"Or like sledding," Linda went on. "Like riding a toboggan down a hill."

I brought the speed up to forty, rounded the next corner, then accelerated to fifty. The engine grew louder. I waited for Linda to object. She didn't, so I continued to increase my speed, touching sixty-five on the speedometer before easing back down for the next curve.

"You okay?" I yelled to Linda.

She didn't answer at first, so I quickly looked over at her.

"Yes!" Her voice screamed out in exhilaration, and though I had looked at her only briefly, I was certain she was smiling, could see the rise of her cheeks beneath her eyes, despite the fact that the helmet covered her mouth. And then I had an idea. I decelerated the car as we approached the entrance to the track, continued to press down gently on the brake until the vehicle had come to a complete stop.

I looked at Linda. She was still smiling. Not saying anything, but still smiling.

I opened my door, got out, and walked around to the passenger side.

Perry had jogged over to the car. "How was it?" he asked.

"Okay," Linda said. "Yes, it was okay." And all the while the smile never left her face.

"That's good," I said, "because now you're going to drive."

"Oh, no," Linda said.

"Oh, yes," I said.

"I can't drive this thing."

"Sure you can," Perry told her. "You don't have to drive it like our Tazmanian Devil here, but you sure as hell can take her out for a spin."

Linda looked forward, at the track, the snow, and the large expanse of lake. Had we pushed her too far?

"I'll do it," she said.

I looked at Perry in disbelief.

"Well, all right then," Perry said.

He took Linda by the elbow and walked her around the vehicle as if he were a bona fide escort. "Little Bit, you going along?" he asked over his shoulder.

"I'll sit this one out," I said. "You go." I took off my helmet and handed it to him.

"I can't fit into your helmet," he said.

"Then switch with Linda," I told him.

Is it fair to say I felt like the parent that day as I stood off to the side and watched my stepmom drive my car around the track? All I know is that I didn't feel like the girl who only two months before had lain on the couch during a snowstorm, waiting for her father to come home. All my life I'd wanted to be taller, bigger. The past two months I hadn't worried about my height, or my hair, or the washed-out pallor of my skin. The past two months I hadn't felt like the daughter, the child. If anything, I had felt lost, as if it wasn't just my father I'd been looking for, but my own self as well. As I watched Linda bring the car up to a steady speed on the straightaway, maybe going as fast as twenty-five or thirty miles per hour, I thought of my reflection in the mirror the morning my father and I had left for Perry's garage. That reflection seemed like a stranger to me now. I had become someone else, and I was beginning to like the person I'd become.

CHAPTER

23

It was Thursday morning, my day off. I slept till seven, when my body could no longer take the cold that was entombing my bones. Two days had passed since Perry and I had taken Linda out on the ice. Did I see a change in her since our outing? I was certain I did. The slightest curl at the corners of her mouth while she vacuumed, a greater efficiency in her actions rather than the slow, clumsy motions of lethargy. More than anything what I think I witnessed was a purpose to her. Maybe I was reading too much into the whole thing. But one thing I was certain of—my own nerves had settled around her. I didn't have that uptight knot in my stomach and sternum. I wasn't carrying with me the fear that she would break.

As I stretched and bounced my legs trying to get my blood moving, I heard the faint voices of the twins and Linda in the kitchen downstairs. "Scott, finish your cereal. You're going to be late." Scott answered, "I *am* finishing it." And then Alex said, "I have a test today." Linda said, "Did you study?"

The three of them bantered back and forth. They sounded like a family, a normal family on a normal day like any other day.

Small feet climbed the stairs. Alex appeared in my doorway. "Will you quiz me?" he asked.

"You have a test?" I asked.

"A spelling test."

"Okay." I sat up, pulling the covers around me.

Alex handed me a piece of paper with twenty words listed.

"Just read them to me, and I'll spell them back," he said, now standing at the foot of my bed.

And so I did, until I came to the word *father*. I hesitated for just a second.

"Father. F-a-t-h-e-r." Alex hadn't waited for my prompt. He knew the order of the words.

Then he said, "It's okay. I know the rest." He took the paper from me and walked toward the door.

"Good luck," I said.

He stopped long enough to say, "It's not luck." He was gone before I could find a response. I wasn't the only one who had changed these past couple of months. So had Alex, and no doubt, so had Scott, as well. I hadn't seen it coming. Even Alex's voice sounded different, not the innocent timbre of a little boy who believed that no wrong or evil could exist. Something about his voice had hardened.

"You're going to miss the bus," I heard Linda say. "Hurry up."

The twins would be leaving in just a few minutes, and by the end of the day, Alex would have grown up a little bit more, and Scott, too. I would never be able to change any of the things that had happened to them, nor would I be able to slow things down or take them back to another time. All I could do was try and make things better.

I climbed out of bed and walked down the hall to take a shower. I knew without really thinking about it what I would be doing that day. I would be driving to Millinocket and looking for Marc Suter because that was something I still had in my power to do. I wanted to set him straight about my dad. Or I wanted to set myself straight. If I could know the truth, hear it from another person, I could answer to people like Eric or anyone else. I hadn't seen Eric since that afternoon in Rockville. I hadn't talked to him either, though he had said he would call. There were three possible reasons why he hadn't called. One, he didn't want to get involved. Two, though his intentions may very well have been good, he might have forgotten to call. And three, he realized that there was *no* truth to any of the things he had said.

Millinocket was about sixty-five miles to the northwest of Sebaticuk. The drive would take me an hour and a half one way. And then there was the possibility that Marc Suter might not be there. What if he was out of town, had taken the day off, or was sick? I wondered if I should try and call ahead. And yet there was something about the element of surprise, about catching him off guard. There was also the fact that I didn't have anything better to do. I would go crazy if I stayed around the house. No, I decided. I would make the drive, find the mill, and hope Suter was clocked in.

Once again, I was in my father's truck, heading out of town. Linda hadn't asked me where I was going. She'd stopped keeping tabs on me once I'd started working full-time. In some ways that made me sad. I could've used a mom checking in on me. But then again, I'd never thought of Linda as a mom anyway. I'd never allowed her that.

It was a clear day, the roads dry with the chalky residue of salt. This would not be the kind of adventure I'd had going up to the logging camp. These highways were well traveled, and the weather forecast showed a three-day window before another storm would set in. The sun beat down on the windshield, heating the inside of the car until I finally rolled down the window, craving the cool air. I would save up for a radio, I decided, one with a CD player. I would play it loud. I tried to remember words to different songs. "Face Down" by Red Jumpsuit Apparatus, and "Photograph" by Nickelback.

Once in Millinocket, I turned off at a BP gas station and went inside to get directions to Devereaux Timber, the place where Marc Suter worked. The woman behind the register wasn't sure. She handed me a phonebook. The lumber company was listed at 3200 Highway 3A. Another customer pointed me down the road, telling me to take a right. I followed his directions with no problem. The lumber company looked like a large hardware store in a metal warehouse. I parked out front and went in.

"Does a man by the name of Marc Suter work here?" I asked the first employee I came to, a lanky, middle-aged woman with cropped hair dyed an orangey red. "Hey, Marc!" she called over her shoulder toward one of the pegboard aisles displaying brackets and hinges.

"Yeah?" An older man walked around the end of the aisle. I guessed him to be somewhere in his late sixties. He had receding silver hair and a rosy nose and cheeks, which, as he drew closer, I identified as a bad case of rosacea. He wasn't tall, maybe five foot seven, and walked with a limp. I hadn't expected to find him so easily, nor had I expected him to look so small and insignificant, grandfatherly in some ways.

"Someone here wants to talk to you," the woman said and walked off.

I was focused on the man approaching me, judging his appearance, the way he walked, trying to determine his character before we'd even spoken.

"Can I help you with something?" he asked.

"I'm Genesis Sommer," I said, my hands remaining in my coat pockets. "I drove up here from Sebaticuk. I wanted to know if I could ask you some questions."

"Sommer." He said my name slowly. His voice had a thin quality to it. "Do I know you?" he asked.

"You may have known my dad. Mike Sommer?"

"*That's* where I know the name." He pointed his finger at me and smiled. "Yes, Mike Sommer."

His smile suddenly faded. Then he laid his hand on my shoulder and steered me around. "Let's go somewhere quiet," he said. "Do you want some coffee or a soda, anything to drink?"

"No, I'm fine."

As we walked, he left his hand on my shoulder for a few seconds longer.

"We'll go back into the employee lounge," he said.

So I followed him toward the back of the warehouse. On our left was a door to a small room with a table, refrigerator, and counter.

Mr. Suter pulled out a chair for me. Then he sat at the other side of the table.

"I am so very sorry about your father," he said. "This must be terrible for you."

I nodded. "It's been rough on all of us," I said.

"How did you get my name? How can I help?"

"It's a long story," I told him.

"Take as long as you need. I'm one of the retired workers around here. I sort of make my own hours."

I nodded, trying to decide where to begin. "I guess what I'd like to know is how you and my father knew each other."

"Oh, gosh." Mr. Suter leaned back in his chair and looked toward the ceiling as if trying to count back through the years. "Let's see. It'd have to be twenty years ago when I first met your dad. I was driving trucks for one of the camps up that way. Used to make some runs for the company he was with. Can't remember the name off the top of my head. Your dad was one of the permanent guys around the camp. He became an old-timer real fast. Most of the men up there don't stay around too long. Get burned out, tired of being away from home."

It was his last comment that bothered me. Was my dad happy to be away from home? "Why do you think my dad stayed at it so long then?" I asked.

"Working for one of the camps gives a guy steady hours and halfway decent pay. That goes a long way when supporting a family. A lot of the other guys drift all over the place, marry several times, drink too much. We got young truckers staying stoned just to get the job done. That's probably one of the biggest reasons I quit. Got tired of sharing the road with them."

Eric had called Suter a drifter, but he didn't sound like a drifter to me. "Do you have any family?" I asked.

"No kids. I had a wife. She passed on a good ten years ago. Got the cancer in her breasts."

"I'm sorry," I said, feeling genuinely sad for him. I thought about asking him if he'd been alone ever since, but it seemed obvious to me that he had. He carried loneliness with him in the way he'd greeted me, helped me with my chair, wanted to take the time to talk with me. There was something about his very presence that welcomed company.

"Was married thirty-five years," he told me.

"That's a long time," I said.

"Yes, it is." He spoke slowly. After a couple of seconds he continued. "We weren't always happy. But we were happy enough. That should count for something."

Mr. Suter was looking at the bare white wall beside us. His mood had suddenly changed. I wondered if my family's loss had reminded him of his own.

"That's something to remember," he told me. "For when you get older. Nobody is ever happy a hundred percent of the time. That's one of life's biggest disappointments, you know. Falling in love and realizing you can't always be happy. But if you're happy enough, then that's something."

I felt calm as Mr. Suter talked. Calm in a way that made me almost forget why I'd come. Calm in a way that I felt like it would be okay if he needed to keep right on talking to me, or to the bare white wall, or even to himself. And when he was done talking, I could get in my truck and drive back home.

He was sad. He missed his wife. Probably when she was alive, he'd never realized just how much he would miss her if she were gone. Maybe when she was alive, he'd had thoughts that he should have married someone else. Maybe her death had changed all of that. Being a child was different. I didn't choose my parents, and because it wasn't a choice, I hadn't invested time in questioning my situation. I'd never said to myself, "Am I happy enough with my father? Should I leave him and find someone else?"

Then Mr. Suter looked at me. "I'm not being much help, am I? I'm sorry for making you put up with my ramblings."

"It's okay," I said.

"What else would you like to know about your dad?" he asked.

I looked at my hands, which were in my lap. I continued to look at my hands as I spoke my next words. "Do you think my father was happy enough?"

Mr. Suter didn't answer right away, so I looked up, meeting his eyes, a dull blue, almost gray, like rain clouds. "Yes, I think he was," he said.

We continued to look at each other. I decided to go on with my questions. "Some people are saying my dad was involved with another woman. Maybe a woman up around the camps. Someone said you might know something."

Mr. Suter's eyes remained fixed on mine. His body remained still. "Your father was a good man," he said.

"So you don't know anything?" I asked.

Again, his eyes remained steadily on mine. "No."

Those weren't Mr. Suter's last words to me, but those were the only words that mattered enough for me not to push my questions any further. We shook hands, and when we did he laid his other hand on my shoulder as if emphasizing the gesture, as if sealing something sacred between us, or maybe just to say, "Thank you for listening." And then again, maybe that was just his way of shaking a person's hand.

I walked out of Devereaux Timber that day in somewhat of a dream state. Maybe it was the sense of release, or maybe it was the exhaustion that had been settling in behind my eyes and into my muscles and even into my lungs. I had accepted my grief. The words sounded harsh, even in the silent recesses of my brain, and yet I knew them to be true.

When I pulled into Sebaticuk, I didn't make the right-hand turn toward the house. Instead I drove down the highway toward the high school. It was almost two thirty. School would be out soon. Then I approached the impound lot, the same lot where my father's truck had first been taken. I pulled up alongside the fence and shifted the truck into park, letting the engine idle. I counted five impound vehicles. M. J. Mahoney's Mercury Cougar was not one of them. I wondered when it had been removed. Had his parents come for it? Had it been sold to a salvage yard or auctioned off? Mahoney had shot himself after returning from the Iraq War. People said he'd suffered from post-traumatic stress disorder. Mike's disappearance was traumatic and stressful. Would Linda or the twins or I suffer from something similar?

Maybe to have PTSD you had to go through something violent. Maybe losing someone you loved wasn't the same thing.

So many thoughts, and all the while I was still staring at the impound lot, the memory of Mahoney like a shadow over every other thought in my mind. Mahoney had taken his life. Had my father done the same? Had he deliberately drowned? My father was a good man, Suter had said. I tried to decide who knew my dad the best. Perry? Linda? Maybe Perry knew parts of him, and Linda knew other parts, and still there were more parts remaining. Just as easily as I'd entertained that question about my dad, I applied it to myself. Who knew me the most? Before my father's disappearance I would have said Annie. Maybe Annie still knew me the most, but wasn't there so much more to me, so many multitudes of thoughts and feelings and intentions and plans and secrets? There was my trip to Millinocket. There was Gabe. There was my guilt because I liked the way Gabe made me feel, because I might be attracted to him. I *was* attracted to him, but my dad was missing and yet I wondered what it would be like to kiss this guy whom I'd recently met, to sit close to him and hold his hand and listen to him tell me facts about things that matter only in encyclopedias or dictionaries.

School would be out soon. Annie would be taking the bus to Big Squaw Mountain for ski practice. I pulled the truck away from the impound lot and drove up the road a ways to the school. Annie's last class was chemistry, in the east wing of the building. No one noticed me enter the school or walk down the hallway to room 136. I waited outside the door. Within minutes the final bell rang. A handful of students spoke to me as they passed. "Hey, how's it going?" Then I saw Annie.

"Gen, what are you doing here?" Annie's eyes widened. She touched me lightly on the arm.

"You got a minute?" I asked.

"Sure. Walk me to my locker."

And so I walked with her to her locker, stood beside her while she put her books away.

"You got ski practice?" I asked, knowing that she did.

"Yeah, but the bus doesn't leave for another twenty minutes. Are you okay?"

"Can we talk?"

"Sure." She closed her locker and the two of us proceeded down the hall to an alcove away from the crowds of students.

"What's up?" she asked.

How long did I look at Annie before I spoke? A couple of seconds maybe, but then I said, "My father's dead." The words felt automatic but also complete. My father was a good man. He'd gone out on his boat. A storm had come up. Maybe his boat had malfunctioned; who was to say? But he was dead, and I knew that as sure as I knew that I was standing before my friend. Did I need to hear myself say those words? Was that why I'd had to find

Annie, to have a witness? Not just say those words, but have them be heard so I couldn't take them back?

Annie slowly raised her fingers to her mouth. "Oh, God, did they find him? Did somebody find his body?" Her eyes glossed over. She cared. Of course she cared.

"No," I said. "No one's found him. I don't know how, and I don't know why, but he's gone. I want so much to bring him back, but I can't."

"It's okay," Annie said.

Her hug wasn't tentative this time. She grabbed me like she might have five years ago. Grabbed me and held me to her like I was the best friend she'd always had, and in that embrace, I felt more than just the shoulders and back of my friend. I felt everything—past, present, future, all bundled up, concentrated into one small space. I wasn't just holding on to Annie. I was holding on to a desire for some sort of promise, for some piece of higher ground in my life, for a place I might imagine.

ICE OUT

CHAPTER
24

Over three months had passed since my trip to Millinocket, since the day I had accepted my grief and my father's death. I tried not to think about what life would be like if he were with us. The idea that struck me was this: life with my dad and life without my dad did not represent a fork in the road, a choice. There was simply one road. This was the greatest change I noticed in myself—my choice to feel alive, and the only way to feel alive was to accept the moment that I was in, and that meant life without my dad. It meant being present in the truest sense. I have no idea how all of this came to me, but it did. Was it because of something Marc Suter had said? Was it because he had told me my dad was a good man? I'd known all along my dad was a good man. Only my fear and pain and my need for my dad to be alive had prevented me from believing in his goodness. The day I met with Marc Suter was the day I could no longer live with the pain that I was, in part, creating for myself. By accepting my grief, accepting the fact that my father had died, I also completely accepted just how much he had loved me, had loved all of us.

He would not be able to watch the twins race their first snowmobiles, or watch Scott pull a dog out of a snowbank and bring him home and name him Rescue, or watch Linda get a job as a receptionist for Maine's Department of Inland Fisheries and Wildlife, working with the very people who had searched for him. But I'm getting ahead of myself. What I'm trying to say is that by accepting what had happened, I had stopped struggling to change things, had stopped the chaos in my head, and was beginning to enjoy the life that still remained.

Other changes had happened as well, significant in their own small way. One night while at Mémère's, I'd asked her to cut my hair. "How short?" she'd asked. "Just below my ears," I'd told her. She'd said, "Are you sure?" And I'd said, "No, but I want you to cut it anyway."

"It changes your face," Linda said after Mémère was finished. "It brings out your eyes. It makes you look older."

Having my hair cut felt symbolic, as if I'd let go of the way things were. Also, I *was* older. Not just older by the fact that several more months had passed. I was now eighteen, officially an adult, even though I had felt like an adult for some time. My birthday had been in March. It wasn't a big celebration. We ate dinner at Mémère's. She made a birthday cake. I was given a new jacket from Perry. Linda and the twins gave me a St. Christopher medallion to wear when I raced. Mémère opened up a savings account for me into which she had deposited a hundred dollars. What I remember most about my birthday were the candles. Before I blew them out, I didn't wish for my father to come home. Instead I wished that I would do something with my life, even though I had no idea what that something might be.

Annie and I saw each other more. Sometimes I'd stop by her house or she'd come into the Lazy Moose just as I'd finish up at work. I can't say things were the way they had been before my father's disappearance. Our friendship had moved on to a new place. It had grown up in some ways, and in other ways it had simply changed because our lives had changed. But all of that was okay, and when we saw each other, like the day at the school when I'd told her my father was dead, I knew that she was okay with everything too. Maybe that was the best thing she gave to the friendship, just letting it be what it was.

As for Gabe, he was another moment my life was in. He was kind, and sometimes nerdy, and sweet, and when I was around him, I no longer thought long and hard about what happened to my dad, or worried about how my family would make it without him. Instead, when I was around Gabe, I enjoyed him. I laughed at the things he said, like when he would start rambling off trivia such as the algorithms for mating fish. And at the same time I'd nod my head, amazed at all of the things he knew. I enjoyed other things about Gabe as well, like the way he'd hold my face, his palms against my cheeks, when I was feeling cold or when he'd look into my eyes just before we'd kiss. Yes, Gabe and I had kissed. The first time was on the lake, about a mile from shore. We were sitting on five-gallon pails in front of his fishing shanty, facing the south, letting the walls of the hut buffer the wind. He leaned toward me as if he were going to whisper something in my ear, but instead he kissed me, his lips cold and chapped, as mine were. We were both hesitant at first, testing the waters so to speak, until we discovered the warmth of each other's mouth and began to relax in that comfort. And when the kiss was over, we looked at each other. "Okay, then," I said.

So that's how it was. We'd talk, we'd listen to each other, and sometimes we'd kiss.

Gabe and I spent a lot of time together, much of which was taking walks on the lake or along cross-country trails. Other times we'd have a meal together at Kelly's Landing. I knew his internship would be up at the end of May and that he'd be returning to Portsmouth, so I didn't allow myself false hopes or fantasies that had to do with the future. I didn't count on a life or even a friendship beyond what I had with him, because if I dared to waste my time with such thoughts, I would miss the very beauty of the moment we were in. This new way of thinking, of being, didn't happen instantaneously. My father had turned up missing in November. Winter had come and gone. The twins had celebrated their birthdays and so had I. Linda's would be next. We'd passed the first day of spring, a snowy day that left another foot of accumulation on the already eighteen inches or so still standing.

Then, the day came when the temperatures warmed up into the forties, and the day after into the fifties. Ever so slowly the snow began to turn to slush, soppy, messy piles of it. Temperatures changed between dull-gray freezing in the morning to teases of warmth in the late afternoons that continued to melt the snow. By late April, mud was everywhere, on the streets, in doorways, on the sides of people's cars. Wet, slick mud. We'd changed our clocks, setting them an hour ahead, and found ourselves eating dinner later and going to bed later as well. The cold was passing and the landscape was changing from brown to green. Kids were on the streets playing catch or shooting baskets and daring summer to come out by wearing shorts, despite the fact that snow still remained in patches along the sides of the roads and in areas of shade.

It was around the middle of May that Gabe and I decided to try for a hike up to the fire tower. The night before, the temperatures had dropped to the teens, freezing the muddy trail cover, allowing us access up the small mountain. Unlike Perry, Gabe had known about the fire tower. He said it was one of ten that had been built in the twenties across the region. However, he'd never climbed it before.

As we reached the metal stairs, I pointed out the osprey nest.

"They're back," he said, pointing just behind us.

Sure enough, against the clear sky, pure and raw and basic, were two ospreys, flying in circles around each other.

"They mate for life," I told Gabe, wanting to be the one to share some knowledge.

"Like swans," Gabe said.

"Not exactly," I said, climbing the stairs.

"How so?"

"Swans *usually* mate for life, but a number of them also split up, especially following a nesting failure."

"I didn't know that," Gabe said.

"So I actually know something you don't," I said, smiling.

Gabe laughed. "Tell me about the ospreys," he said as we continued to climb.

"The ospreys seem to depend on each other, even beyond their mating and their parenting."

Once we were inside the cab at the top of the tower, we immediately felt the cold air whipping in through the openings. Gabe stood behind me and wrapped his arms around my shoulders so that my body was pressed against his. "Do you ever think about finishing up school?" he asked. "Going to college?"

"I think about it," I said. "I probably thought about it more before my dad went missing."

"It's not impossible, you know."

"I don't know."

"Seriously, Gen. That's why there's government grants and student loans. You wouldn't even have to finish high school. You could take the GED."

"Maybe now's just not the time to think about it."

"Okay," he said.

And so we stood there together, looking out over the treetops and the lake beyond. We stood there in a space of silence, something we'd gotten used to over the past two months, a space in which we might hear each other, as well as hear ourselves better.

And then I said, "Maybe soon."

And he said, "Okay," again.

Of course I had thought about taking classes, of going to college. My birthday wish had been to do something with my life, to move on. But there were others to consider as well. There were Linda and the twins. And then Gabe said something that triggered a feeling of possibility in me.

"There's so much balance out here."

"What do you mean?" I asked.

"The whole habitat thing. The fish mass multiply. The ospreys eat the fish. They have two or three, maybe four offspring. They live a long time. The fish don't live as long, but they breed more, and so it's okay. I'm simplifying, I know. And then there's the whole flora balance as well, and the balance of the seasons."

"It's not all one thing or another," I said.

"Keep talking," Gabe said.

"Well, it's like I want to be there for my family. I want to help. But I also want to be there for myself. It's about balance. Take going to college, for example. Maybe I can't up and leave everyone behind. Maybe I wouldn't even want to do that. But I could maybe start the process. Sign up for a class or two, balance the whole thing out."

"Of course you could," Gabe said. "You may have to drive a ways, but there's a couple of options within an hour or so of here."

Gabe held me tighter, kissed my cheek, kept his face close to mine. I was staring out at the lake.

"Hey, Gabe, do you have your binoculars?" I asked.

"Yeah, they're in my pocket."

He let go and unzipped the side pocket of his parka, then handed them to me.

I glassed Otter Cove and the surrounding area.

"See something?" he asked.

"Take a look," I said, handing him the binoculars. "The ice is breaking up."

Small black patches, resembling oil spills, appeared at different points on the lake.

"I'd say within another week there will be a number of clear channels." Gabe still held the binoculars to his face.

Ice out typically happened mid-May, give or take a couple of weeks. It was thought to be the date of open navigation from Sebaticuk to the Northeast Carry River.

"If we get another warm trend, maybe ninety percent of the lake will be clear," Gabe added.

And then I said something that surprised me. "He's been silent for so long."

Was I thinking that despite accepting my father's death, his voice would arise from the newly exposed water, that the ice had trapped his spirit, kept him in some kind of limbo like a purgatory?

"What do you think he would say?" Gabe asked. He was holding my hand. I didn't remember him taking my hand in his, but there we were, standing together, as I thought about my dad.

"I don't know. Maybe something peaceful. He'd tell me not to worry."

"*Pax vobiscum*," Gabe said.

"Do you go to church?" I asked.

"I used to."

"Me too. Do you remember hearing the words, 'Lo, I am with you always'?"

"Yes."

I hesitated for just a second, tasting a hint of pine in the air. I continued to look out over the lake, searching for the places of open water with my naked eye. "That's what I imagine he would say to me now."

CHAPTER
25

I didn't feel it coming. Didn't experience a throbbing pulse beneath my skin or a jolt of sadness. It was a day like any other day. I awoke at five, showered, and drove to work. I parked behind the diner, got out. I was a few minutes early as I usually was, so I walked around the restaurant to Main Street and looked out over the lake. The water was calm. Ice patches were scant, resembling pearls on a floating necklace. The sky was almost blue. I looked at my watch. I still had a few minutes before I had to show up for my shift. I'd grown to like the early mornings, the timid light, the customers with bed creases on their skin, the smell of frost and earth. I took in a deep breath, held it for as long as I could until my head began to hurt. I let the air out slowly, turned around, and walked toward the restaurant.

Dorrie was waiting for me just inside the back door. "Gen," she said. And then she hugged me. She smelled of hair perm and something sweet.

"What is it?" I asked.

"Officer Whalen's here."

"Where is he?"

"Out front. He's waiting for you."

I'm sure I hesitated for a couple of seconds, hesitated long enough to register what she was telling me, but all I remember is saying, "No, where's my dad?"

As I pulled away, Dorrie's fingers held on to my arms. "I'll get Officer Whalen," she said.

I didn't feel the next couple of minutes pass. I wasn't asleep, yet I don't remember anything either. One minute Dorrie was squeezing my arms. The next minute I was sitting in a chair beside the counter and Officer Whalen was sitting in a chair in front of me. I smelled bacon and sausage. People were out front ordering breakfast, talking, drinking coffee. I was listening to Officer Whalen.

"I'm sorry, Gen. I hate to have to tell you this. But we've found him."

The griddle popped with grease. The counter was silver and shiny. A glint of light reflected off of it from Officer Whalen's watch. "Where?" I asked.

"Black Point. Other side of Otter Cove. He'd washed up on shore. A guy spotted him this morning."

"Who?"

"A man from out of town."

"I want to see my dad," I said.

"There's a team there now. They haven't moved him yet."

"Will you take me there?"

Officer Whalen raised his hand and gently pressed it against the side of my head. "Yes."

"What about Linda? Does she know?"

"Perry's on his way to the house."

"How long ago did this guy find him?"

"Maybe an hour. The sheriff had to identify him first."

I stood up. I walked to the door. Suddenly I felt light-headed and grabbed the edge of the counter for support. Officer Whalen moved forward to reach for me.

"No, I'm okay," I said.

Officer Whalen led me out of the restaurant to his car. He knelt beside me after I climbed in.

"Are you sure you want to go out there?" he asked.

"Yes. I have to see him."

"It's been over six months. He won't look good. I just want to prepare you."

"I know," I said.

I had accepted that my father wasn't coming back. I had accepted that he had died. And yet nothing could have prepared me for that morning.

Memories, so many of them, mixed together, creating a sort of kaleidoscope image in my mind. My seven-year-old birthday party—the cake my dad had tried to make, the party hat he had worn. The sight of his face appearing around the edge of my bedroom door when he would check in on me late at night, the way his big body rocked behind a grocery cart when we'd shop together before he and Linda had married, the way he wore the front of his flannel shirt tucked in but the back of his shirt pulled out, the way he looked at me before he left Perry's garage the day he disappeared.

If Officer Whalen said anything, I didn't hear him. Nor did I hear his radio. I might as well have slipped into another world.

And then we were there, pulling up toward the shore, driving along a muddy side road from the highway, rocks and dirt kicking up beneath the tires. All before me the sky was the color of bleached-out denim. A cluster of people were standing along the water's edge. There were police cars nearby and an ambulance. An ambulance, as if my father might still be able to be saved.

I didn't wait for Officer Whalen. I opened my door, stepped out of the vehicle, and began walking toward the small crowd. A couple of people saw me. They moved aside. And then I saw him, my father's body. He wasn't lying on his back. He was on his side, facing me, his arms pulled up in front of him as if he were sleeping, almost covering his face, his skin the color of a new bruise, the color of death and cold.

I knelt beside him and touched his hair, still thick and blond, its texture now that of frost. The lake had preserved him well. His eyes were closed and I could only wonder when they had shut. Had he closed them when he'd fallen into the water? Had his heart stopped beating while he was still on the boat? I realized that none of that mattered. This was the body of my father, the body that had held his life for all of his forty-two years, the same body that had held me when. I was small and afraid, and had swung me around when he was proud.

I didn't cry then. Strange, perhaps. But seeing his body, I knew that his life was somewhere else, knew it as strongly as I knew love or joy or the kind of security I'd known when I'd been with my dad. At that moment I felt my father's presence, not in the physical being in front of me, but around me, like a soft blanket over my shoulders.

"I love you," I said.

And then I stood. Officer Whalen was the first person I saw. Everyone else was just a blur, just faces and jackets that didn't belong.

"Where will they take him?" I asked.

"They'll move him to the hospital and wait for your family to make arrangements."

My family. Me and Linda and Perry and Mémère.

"I don't want my brothers to see him," I said.

"I can understand."

I turned and walked back to the car. Before I got in, I looked over my shoulder, not at the body that lay on the shore, but at the large mass of water that had taken so much from my life.

Officer Whalen started the car.

"It will never be the same," I said.

"No."

"It will be different."

"I know."

"Okay, then."

CHAPTER
26

I dreamed of Mt. Kineo, its massive cliffs rising out of the black water. Was it a sign? Was my father trying to tell me something? I don't think so. Instead I recognized the dream as my own voice telling me that Mt. Kineo was where my father's ashes should be spread. Linda and Mémère had talked of spreading Dad's ashes in the water, and I had said no. Why would we want to give his ashes to the very body of water that had taken his life? "Where then?" Linda had asked.

"I don't know, but not in the lake," I said.

Then I had the dream. Thoreau had referred to Mt. Kineo as "that rough tooth in the sea." My father had told me that the mountain was a tribute to the great queen of the moose tribe who had been hunted and killed. He'd pointed out the shape of the mountain, showing me how it resembled the back and head of a moose. But more than any of that, what I saw in the mountain was a place where my father had hiked at one time or another with all of us.

The morning I woke from the dream, I shared my idea with Linda. "Yes," she said. We were sitting at the kitchen table. She took my hand and held it while she finished her coffee. She would do that from time to time when her memories of my father would take over. She'd reach for my hand, and I'd see the look in her eyes change, her focus disappear. I'd know then that she was reliving a moment she had shared with my dad. I'd see the same look in Perry or Mémère from time to time. Perhaps they saw it in me, as well.

We'd had a memorial service for my father at the church a week after his body had been found. But that's not what I chose to remember. Instead I chose to think of a day in June when the sun was warm and the sky was clear and we took a ferry to the north end of the lake to Mt. Kineo. It was the first time since my father's disappearance that any of us had been on a boat. Aside from the operator of the ferry, there were just the seven of us: me, Linda, Mémère, Perry, Scott, Alex, and Rescue, the small black dog that Scott had pulled out of the snowbank.

In Greek, the word *kineo* means "move," one of the many points of trivia Gabe had shared with me. It's that word, *move*, that I associated so strongly with our day on Mt. Kineo. Our coming together so that we could move on.

I had several images from that day, like clips from a movie reel, and when I put them together, they formed something that felt almost complete. The first of those images is that of my family as we took the ferry over to the peninsula, the roundish mass of land that, except for its narrow isthmus on its northeast edge, felt more like an island. The ride took only about twenty minutes, and the boat that carried us over didn't feel a whole lot bigger than my father's Thompson. Scott and Alex sat at the bow, just in front of the steering well, their bodies turned so that they were facing the lake, the spray of water dampening their faces. Each of them had an arm around Rescue, who was perched between them, his eyes squinting against the wind and his tongue lapping at the misty air. We were on a mission. We were going to spread the ashes of our father. Scott and Alex knew what we were there to do, and yet, as I looked at their faces, there was something playful in their eyes, something playful in the way they held on to their newest pride possession, a black bundle of fur. Scott pointed out a boat and said something to Alex, who nodded and said something back, their voices drowned out by the boat's motor, the chopping of the hull against the small waves, the cutting wind from the boat's speed.

What I saw were two boys with a dog, two boys who would return home that day smelling of fresh air and sweat and something earthy and musky from the soil on their jeans. What I didn't see was a funeral, an end, two boys withdrawn into grief. Instead their eyes were wide, their mouths slightly open as they took in the lake air. And then I realized they were laughing at something one of them had said, or maybe at something Rescue had done.

They were in a world separate from the one in which we had existed for so long—the one without our father.

Alex shook his head back and forth in front of Scott's face, sending droplets of water from his hair onto Scott's cheeks. Then Scott did the same, until they both bumped heads. Scott said something cross and buffed Alex on the shoulder and Rescue barked, no doubt thinking he should be part of the whole game. Then they were laughing again.

The next image was that of us hiking the trail that wrapped around the back side of the mountain to the top. A large stretch at the base followed along the water's edge. The twins ran ahead of us about fifty yards, with Rescue chasing them, to a rocky beach. They scooped up handfuls of stones and began a contest to see who could throw the farthest. Rescue waded into the water and swam toward the splashes, attempting to retrieve whatever it was that was being tossed.

"Nice one!" Mémère yelled.

"Did you see that?" Scott said. "That was at least thirty yards."

"No way!" Alex yelled. "Watch this."

Then Perry joined them. "Yeah, but who can skip it the most times?" He bent over and began looking for rocks with smooth, flat surfaces.

Within minutes all of us were searching for the *perfect* rock to skip, even Mémère, who had been carrying the wooden box that held my father's ashes. She set the box beneath one of the spruce trees along the shore, walked to the water's edge, and stooped over with her hands held together behind her back.

"Here's one, Alex," she said, reaching over to pick it up.

"Let me see," Scott said.

Rescue was now standing on the shore, shaking his coat furiously, which immediately set the twins into hearty squeals and laughter. Even Linda was laughing as she held up her arms over her face against the spray.

"Watch this," Perry said, bringing his arm around in full motion and letting a rock slide from his hand. We all counted as the stone brushed the surface eight times.

"Holy cow! Let me try." Next it was Alex. Then Scott. Then Linda. Mémère and I took our turns as well. I think I skipped one seven times. Mémère maybe three, and Linda five. We were standing on the water's edge, tossing and skipping stones and looking for more stones. I didn't think about my father at that moment, didn't think about his ashes in the box beneath the tree behind us. I thought only about trying to skip a stone as far as I could, something like pure freedom in that competitive, repetitious act.

The rest of the hike took us about an hour and a half, the trail eventually turning into steep switchbacks, often-times obstructed with boulders and large slabs of horn-stone. "You okay, Mom?" Perry would stop to ask. "Fine," Mémère would say.

"Scott, be careful! Don't get so close to the edge," Linda yelled.

I was following behind Mémère. Perry stopped in front of us. "Let me take that," he said, reaching for the box. But Mémère insisted, "No, I got it." I guess the way Mémère saw it was that it was she who had brought my father into the world, and it would be she who would let his ashes go.

. . .

This is what I remember. All of us standing at the top of the sixty-foot fire tower at the highest point on Mt. Kineo. The base was constructed of steel, with open stairs. The top was a wooden platform with a steel railing. Like many of the fire towers around the state, it had been built in the early part of the century. Throughout the years different groups had restored it. Each of us had climbed the fire tower with my dad at one time or another. And somewhere back at the house, there were pictures from different family outings to Kineo. I would look for those photos later. I would dig through boxes obsessively until I found the one of my dad and me that Linda had taken when I was ten, the two of us standing together on the tower. But that would come later.

As we stood together that day, our chatter subsided. I listened to the wind whistle around us, heard the faint rustle of our clothes, though we were each standing still.

"Well then," Mémère said. She opened the box and took out the bag that held Dad's ashes. Perry took the box from her and set it on the platform.

Mémère stepped closer to the railing, embracing the clear plastic bag against her chest. "Mon Dieu, take care of my son," she said, her voice catching in her throat.

"It's okay, Mémère." Scott walked over beside her and dipped his small, freckled hand into the bag. After a couple of seconds, he pulled out a fistful of the ashes. He extended his arm over the railing and ever so slowly opened his palm. The heavier particles fell toward the ground, but the finer ashes were carried by the breeze.

Then Perry reached inside the bag, and then Alex. Perry held his hand open over the railing as Scott had, but Alex threw his as if tossing a rock or a ball. I watched his face. Was he angry? Sweat glistened beneath his eyes, but he wasn't crying. Maybe he was simply trying to let go of all the grief as we all had been. I looked to Linda. She wasn't crying either. She looked peaceful, resolved, staring out over the lake, following the swirls of fine dust with her eyes.

"Shall we join them?" she asked Mémère. And then she, too, reached her hand into the bag, as did Mémère, their fingernails scraping against the plastic. Linda was standing beside me. She took my hand, opened up my fingers, and holding her fist just above my palm, sifted some of the particles onto my skin. "He loved you, Gen."

I clutched my fingers around the ashes, held them for a few seconds before tossing them into the air. "I know," I said. "He loved all of us."

AUTHOR'S NOTE

Season of Ice originated with a place that tapped into
something nostalgic from my childhood. My father's
family is from the Upper Peninsula of Michigan, where
many of the men worked as commercial fishermen. Some
of my fondest memories are of the vacations I spent in
the UP. I loved the lake, the woods, the time with my
family, and the whole physical way of life captured in
that setting. Then, several years ago I traveled to northern Maine, where I camped and kayaked along Moosehead Lake. I felt an affinity for the terrain and the people
and knew I wanted to write a novel that took place in
that part of the country. I had the privilege of returning
to Moosehead Lake the following winter to write an article on a teenage ice car racer, Nikki Hamilton. I was
again drawn intimately to the area. When I returned to
Colorado, where I was then living, I began creating a
character for a new novel. I wanted her to be much like
Nikki, but I wasn't yet sure what her story would be.

Over the course of the year, several events came

together that shaped the story and the life of my character, Genesis Sommer. One afternoon I received the sad call from my grandmother that my cousin Andy had disappeared after having gone out on his boat for a fishing trip. His boat had been found, but not his body. Andy had grown up on the water. He understood boats; he was a strong swimmer. The search for my cousin continued, and eventually his body was found. Not long after my cousin's death, a man in Colorado went missing. He had been cross-country skiing with his family when the group became disoriented during a snowstorm. His wife, daughter, and dog had stayed together, while the man ventured off to find help. After two days, everyone except for the man was found. The search for the skier continued, but it was eventually called off because of heavy snowfall. Search-and-recovery efforts were to resume the following spring.

The grief my family felt for my cousin, along with the story of the missing skier, weighed heavily on me. One night while hiking in the snow, I thought about what would happen if a person went missing on a lake, and in the midst of the search for the person, the lake froze over. As with the skier's situation, efforts would be delayed until ice out, when the lake thawed. I thought about what the family would go through, the rumors that might be spread in a small town, how the family would survive without any life insurance. I returned home that evening, built a fire, and began writing this novel. As the story took form on the pages, I felt the ice cover of my own life, an incubation of sorts. My life was also changing in a dramatic way. I was about to leave an area I had called home for almost fourteen years and start a new life where I did not know anyone.

A friend once told me, "Life never gives you Plan A. It's how well you deal with Plan B that matters." A novel is a work of fiction, and yet it is inspired by human truth. I think of so many families whose life courses have taken dramatic and unexpected turns. With *Season of Ice* I have tried to capture such a family, especially giving voice to a young woman who, despite the changes in her life, has discovered how to live.

ACKNOWLEDGMENTS

I am deeply appreciative to the community of Greenville, Maine, and all of those who provided me with information needed to write this novel. Many thanks especially to the talented young ice car racer Nikki Hamilton, who answered my endless questions; to her father, Kirk, who put me in touch with others in the community and helped me to understand the logging industry, as well as the position of a delimber. Thanks to Tony Cirulli, who introduced me to Nikki; to Nikki's uncle Perry, who let me drive his car in a racing heat; to the people at Flatlanders, Boom Chain, Stress Free Moose, Woody's, Wilsons, and Northwoods Outfitters for the meals and coffee and conversation; to Dennis and Sharon Curtis for their cabin and for letting me borrow their outboard; to the wardens and staff of Maine's Inland Fisheries and Wildlife, especially Adam Gormely. I am deeply indebted to search pilot Brad Randall and to auto-mechanic extraordinaire Craig White. Thanks to

Jeannine Pelletier for her help with the French Canadian phrases; to Uncle Dale and to Joe VanRemortel for their help with the boating information; to Great Northern, and especially to Dan at the 5th St. John Camp, who gave me a tour and explained the camp's operations. I am extremely grateful to my friends at Stonecoast MFA for their continued encouragement; to Southern New Hampshire University for its unfailing support; to Dean Karen Erickson; to mentor and friend, Bob Begiebing, MFA director; and to all of my colleagues in the School of Liberal Arts. Thank you to the New Hampshire Writer's Project, and to its executive director, Barbara Yoder, for arranging readings for me; to poet Baron Wormser and his wife, Janet, for providing company and guidance when I needed it most. A special thanks to the PEN American Center for its recognition of my work and to Phyllis Naylor for her financial support via the fellowship. As always, thanks to my agent, Steven Chudney, and to my editor, Melanie Cecka, who believed in the novel after having read only four pages, and who remained consistently supportive not only of the novel but also of the author. Thank you to my friends in Colorado—I could never say enough good things about them—I have been blessed. I will forever be grateful to my family and my sons—throughout life's changes their love has remained constant. Thank you to my oldest son, Nate, for all of his help and strength throughout our first year in New Hampshire. And lastly I am deeply grateful to author and friend Michael White, who first introduced me to Moosehead Lake and whose work and love inspired my writing and life to a higher ground. Thank you for being there every step of the way.